SMOG

ISABELLE LLASERA

Published by Cinnamon Press
Meirion House, Tanygrisiau, Blaenau Ffestiniog,
Gwynedd, LL41 3SU
www.cinnamonpress.com

The right of Isabelle Llasera to be identified as author of this work has been asserted by her in accordance with the Copyright, Designs and Patent Act, 1988. © 2020 Isabelle Llasera.

Print Edition ISBN 978-1-78864-103-6

British Library Cataloguing in Publication Data. A CIP record for this book can be obtained from the British Library.

All rights reserved. No part of this publication may be reproduced, stored in a retrieval system, or transmitted in any form or by any means, electronic, mechanical, photocopying, recording or otherwise without the prior written permission of the publishers. This book may not be lent, hired out, resold or otherwise disposed of by way of trade in any form of binding or cover other than that in which it is published, without the prior consent of the publishers.

Designed and typeset in Garamond by Cinnamon Press. Cover image, 'Brovès', by Adam Craig. Cover design by Adam Craig.

Cinnamon Press is represented by Inpress and by the Books Council of Wales.

The publisher gratefully acknowledges the support of the the Books Council of Wales.

Acknowledgments

'Muse' won a prize in the 2013 Segora short story competition. 'The Madman' was first published in 2014 by HISSAC in HISSAC winners, an anthology of short stories. 'Ruins', 'The Van', 'That Girl', 'Annie' and 'The Footstool and the Suitcase' were first published in 2017 by Cinnamon Press in Ruins, an anthology. 'Smog' and 'Rear View' were first published in 2018 by Cinnamon Press in The Cinnamon Review of Short Fiction.

I would like to thank my first readers, Anna Pook, Rosemary Milne, Martin Raim and Pamela Shandel for their inspiration, enthusiasm and friendship over the years; Rowan Fortune for his patience, advice and encouragement, and all at Cinnamon, especially Adam Craig and Jan Fortune for the wisdom of their boldness and for their unwavering support and generosity.

CONTENTS

Rear View	7
Dan Blavet	18
Muse	31
It's Me	39
Last Time	48
John's Your Man	61
At the Bottom of the Garden	67
The Footstool and the Suitcase	77
Smog	89
The Van	99
That Girl	112
Annie	122
The Madman	130
Ruins	136

SMOG

Rear View

The first time he met Yolande's eyes, in the rear-view mirror of his taxi, Yves crashed into the Volvo in front. It was drizzly at the Gare de Lyon. He'd shoved her bags in the boot, held the back door while she settled and taken his place behind the wheel.

'Where to?'

She gave an address in the 11th. There was a quiver in her voice. It made her sound like a child swallowing a sob, or a giggle. He shot a glance at the mirror, caught her eyes, gleaming under her red fringe, pressed on the gas and slammed into the Volvo. After a brief exchange of insults and documents with the Volvo driver, Yves got back in and looked up at the mirror. She was smiling, staring at the streaks of rain trickling down the windscreen.

'Sorry about this. What's the address again?'

He didn't start the engine this time. He sat back and inhaled a faint scent of vanilla as the quiver mingled with the soft pit pat on the car roof. When the taxis behind started hooting, he put the wipers on slow and took the long way round to the 11th, glancing at the mirror all the while. A couple of months later, he'd left his small suburban flat and moved in with Yolande.

Yves moaned about life in the city. How you lost touch with the bigger picture when stuck in a traffic jam or have to watch out for bikes, cars and buses before stepping off a pavement. The way you're trapped in the here and now by neighbours walking in high heels above your head or drilling holes in the wall behind your bed. Restrained and stifled, you're robbed of time and horizon in a city.

They talked and talked about leaving Paris. He told Yolande about a place he knew in the purple-blue mountains of the south east. He'd gone for a summer cycling tour of the country with Sam and Georges, his two pals, at the end of their two-year apprenticeship in carpentry. Once they'd pitched their tent in those mountains, they declared it was paradise and stayed till the end of their holiday. Lying on a smooth rock at night, smoking weed and counting shooting stars, splashing in a cool stream when they woke, and watching vultures gliding in the currents of the wind were memories Yves conjured up and clung to whenever he felt walled in. He knew a place where your gaze could drift off, your mind take height and where mountains, beasts and people fitted. At night, sometimes, he held Yolande's hand and trilled and hooted the way he'd heard blackbirds and night owls do out there.

'That's where I'd like to be,' he whispered.

On the night of 13th November, 2015, as the sirens wailed in the street below and they sat watching the carnage on the telly, Yves said, 'It's now or never. Let's pack the bags and go.' Eyes glued to the box and oozing tears, Yolande, who until now wasn't sure, slowly nodded. He sold his taxi licence, she handed in her notice to the post office sorting centre and, as poppies were starting to bloom in the fields, they settled in a small wooden house in the shade of the mountain where he'd spent that summer, more than two decades earlier.

Yves steps out onto the terrace, stretches and yawns. If Bruno's van wasn't in his driveway, he'd howl. He howls in the morning when Bruno's gone. Loosens the throat, clears the lungs and prepares you to face the day like a newborn baby thrown into the world. What's the point in living in the wilds if you can't holler when you feel the need, he tells Yolande.

The dogs rush out from their kennel, stretch and yap. He'll take them for a walk after breakfast, across the stream and up to the glade, his favourite spot. If he has no job to do in the village, he sits on a rock, pulls his knife from his pocket and carving a frog or an owl out of a fallen pine branch, makes guesses at the twitters and swishes he hears. As the sun rises and the trees light up, the blue layers of mountains lose colour and turn to misty hills towards the south. Beyond them, the mist blends with the silver expanse of the sea and, across it, he imagines Africa. The world doesn't seem that huge from up there, as if continents and oceans were at hand, because it's easy to picture them when you're on a mountain top in the stillness of the morning. Plus, you can howl like a lone wolf baying at the moon and no one, not even the sheep, will give a fig.

Bruno whistles down his front steps and Yves makes a quick retreat inside. The twit whistles in the morning when he leaves to empty shitty pipes and rotting drains. He whistles when he comes back. He whistles on Sundays when he potters round his garden. *Hello, le soleil brille, brille, brille,* or some such ancient military crap. A door slams and Yves watches from the window as Bruno's van disappears behind the pines. He steps back out onto the terrace and howls. Glancing at the rear-view mirror fixed on the terrace banister, he catches a glimpse of Yolande coming out of the bathroom in her bra and knickers.

She's off to give her country dance class. He's stopped going. He knows the steps. They sometimes put a record on in the evening and tap, slide, stomp right and left to celebrate a day of bold blue sky, or a couple of roe deer, two the hunters' bullets didn't get, stealing across the field at dusk for a drink at the stream. He'll go to one or two rehearsals before the show for the *Restos du Coeur* day in March, just to make sure the old birds in the group wear their cowboy hats at the right angle and keep in line with him. He'd rather walk the dogs up to the glade, squint towards the hills and whittle out a swallow or a squirrel. If he has no job to do in the village, that is.

He had a card made soon as they arrived. 'New in the area. Self-employed Jack of all trades, Yves redecorates houses, puts up shelves, prunes trees, etc.' Before long, he had a shed to build, a bathroom to paint, kitchen tiles to change, cupboards to fit. But offers began to drop in the summer down, in September, to watering two elderly ladies' gardens every other day, then to chopping their wood for the winter. Nothing so far this month. He hasn't told Yolande. But he's got this big job coming in Castel, a second home the guy wants redecorated. He went round, reckoned it was a five or six-week job and gave an estimate. 'Fine,' the guy said. 'When can you start?' After he'd emailed him the detailed estimate that night, Yves cracked open a bottle of good wine and whisked Yolande off the sofa for a few steps.

'See you tonight!' She blows him a kiss from the door and swirls out in red white and blue jeans and star-spangled cowboy boots, leaving a whiff of vanilla hanging in the air. He goes to the sink to rinse their cups and glances at the mirror he's fixed above the drainer. Bruno's van's parked further down the lane. He tilts the mirror to get a better view. Yolande's leaning on the twit's open window. When she finally steps back, she waves in the direction of the van as it disappears. He goes to the window. She's starting her Clio. He must put an extra mirror in the living room as well as fix a couple in the room upstairs.

Yves started having eyes at the back his head in his first year at secondary school. His mum had given him an old plastic vanity case to put his pencils in. It had a small mirror stuck on the inside of the lid. With the box open and well placed, he could peep at the fair-haired little twerp who sat behind him and whispered *bougnoule* down his neck when he could get his desk close enough. And he shouted *bicot* running past him in the playground. Yves looked the words up in the dictionary and learned what *Péj.* meant. 'Go back to your country,' the twerp and a friend of his threw at him when he was the last to leave the gym and at the school gate once, walking on either side of Yves, sticking their elbows in his ribs.

During a history test, Yves glanced at the little mirror in his pencil case and caught goldilocks unfolding a small piece of paper and copying from it. He broke into a sweat. He knew something no one else knew, something he could use, a weapon of sorts, better than fists, stone or knife, as there'd be no visible trace if he flung it at his face. A week later, the teacher gave back the tests. The twerp had one of the top marks and the teacher's congrats. At the canteen, as goldilocks was turning away from the queue carrying his tray, Yves stood in front of him, heart racing, and hissed: 'Hi there, teacher's pet. Getting all your answers right all of a sudden, hey? Aw. You must be so proud of yourself, you big-arsed shitty cheat. So proud.' He quickly turned and left, but never heard another insult from the bully after that. He kept that pencil case till he left school.

Yves calls the dogs, takes long strides across the field, fords the stream and starts up the mountain, Coyote sniffing by his side, Cheyenne rushing in and out of the undergrowth. There's plenty of room for memories to bubble up when you've got unwanted time on your hands and nothing to grip your mind. Memories slipping back to when he, Sam and Georges were sacked from the furniture company they'd been working at for twelve years. The boss had got the seven employees together, told them labour costs were too high, orders were dwindling, no one had offered to buy the business back and he was forced to close down. They'd been used and thrown on the scrapheap like broken tools. 'Not like my dad', he says out loud, kicking at a stump on the path. His dad, with a job for life—forty-four years of laying tracks around the country, levelling ballast, placing sleepers, tightening, loosening, lifting, loading, wedging, welding.

'Hiya, throwaway guy. Fancy a game of pinball?' Yves, Sam and Georges gave each other a punch on the shoulder when they met at the local café. They shared a beer or two. They signed on at the job centre and filled in forms. They scratched lottery cards. They wrote and rewrote their CVs, sent them to all the kitchen fitters, joiners, sawmills and furniture firms, first around the capital and then the country. They had a bar code tattooed at the base of their necks.

'Want a price etched above the bar code?' the guy asked.

'No,' they said, 'we're way too expensive for anyone to buy us. Pricey throwaways.'

Six months later, Georges got a job in Lorraine, then Sam a job in Normandy. Yves had sent his CV to eighty-four different companies over the year, had five interviews and not a single offer. The woman at the job centre told him he'd better change strategies. His CV was fine but should be revamped. His name, not Yves of course, but his surname, might put employers off. As well, as a matter of fact, as his photo. And unfortunately, 9-3, his post code, and Saint-Denis, his place of birth and residence, had a bad reputation. As a result, they shouldn't appear. The anonymous CV was the new thing.

'Have I got this right?' he asked the woman. 'You mean I have to hide who I am because who I am might upset a bloke who happens to be a boss? What if I don't like the looks of the boss? What if I don't fancy his name? What if his address stinks of mega pimping, tax dodging and god knows what else and it makes me sick?' They'd ditched him and, now, they wanted him invisible. He gave the woman the finger, never set foot in the job centre again and, with the help of his mum and dad, bought a taxi licence and chose the night shift.

No one had objected to his dad's name, address and dark features when they came to fetch him and hundreds of others, in their remote Atlas villages, to expand the French railway network in the early 1970s. And when his dad retired last year, he got a short speech from the foreman, a few crisps on a plastic plate, a Styrofoam cup of fizzy juice, and half his French colleagues' pension. But, damn it, Yves's not Moroccan. Conceived and produced in France he was, not long after his dad fell for a young girl from Brittany who sold tickets at the Gare Montparnasse.

But for shit's sake, he didn't come here to think about his dad and mull over the past, or retire and roam the mountains all day. He reaches the fork half way up to the glade and looks down towards the village. The English flag in front of Denis's house is at half mast. He's heard Denis hoists it at full mast when the weed's outstanding, low when none's available. He spots Denis busy putting out his junk in front of his garage. He may have one or two old rear-view mirrors to sell. Yves calls the dogs and takes the path down to the village.

'Why an English flag?' he asks Denis.

'Cos they think I'm a weird old Brit come to retire in Provence, celebrating weird old Brit anniversaries, and they let me be. If I put the French flag up, the bums in the county'd think I'm *Front National* and they'd come tagging swastikas on my front door at night,' Denis explains as he places battered saucepans, chipped China saucers and old *Paris Match* magazines on a blanket.

Yves buys twenty grams of weed and decides to drive down to Castel. Images of swastikas sitting next to the French flag stick to his mind like grains of sand to an open wound. He punches the wheel and steps on the gas like he's late for something. He hoots at cyclists, zooms down a bend, nearly veers off the road. Just before Castel, he slows down and glances at the guy's big house.

Bruno's van's parked in front. He stops in the shade of a row of cypress trees, peeps through a gap between the branches. The guy's coming out of his house. Goldilocks is behind him. Not that Bruno has girly curls like the little bastard who pops in Yves's mind for the first time since his school days. No, Bruno's got a solid crew cut, like a copper helmet on his head. They're talking, gesturing, nodding. They're shaking hands. Looks like a deal all right. Yves undoes the handbrake, lets the car glide down into a field, stops behind a hedge and rolls himself a joint as he watches Bruno get into his van and drive away. In Castel, he buys a pack of beers, sits on a bench, knocks back two cans and smokes another joint. He walks past a tattoo salon, goes in.

'Made in France,' he says tapping the base of his neck. 'Just below the bar code.'

'A price inked in?'

'It'd have to be a row of noughts then. But no. Thanks. Nothing.'

'Priceless, hey?'

He shows Yolande in the evening. 'You never know,' he says. She shakes her head, pushes him onto the sofa and curls up against him. She rolls the hair down his neck around her fingers and plants a kiss on 'Made in France'.

'Who cares where you were made.'

'Everyone.'

'Well I don't. And I don't know what you're talking about.'

There's this childish streak in Yolande. She sees the world through rose-tinted glasses. She says money spoils the world. She gives the country dance classes for free, volunteers to look after the tiny local library two mornings a week. She picks up cans rolling about in the street and throws them in a bin. She says there's just one human race. She sends money to charities, drops coins in the cups of guys sleeping rough. As if any of it ever really changed a thing.

After she's gone to the library the next day, Yves checks his emails. 'Thanks for the estimate but the job can't be done. Sorry.' He calls the guy in his big house in Castel.

'Sorry,' the guy repeats, 'but I'm not doing it.' And he hangs up. No explanation. Nothing. Just, it's no go.

So Bruno's got the job and not just the plumbing. But Bruno's not acting on the sly. He's no cheat like the little bastard at school. He only got the job Yves didn't get. And Yves will hear him whistle down his steps every fucking winter morning.

How will he tell her? How will he explain to Yolande why the guy's changed his mind? Why the only jobs he's had since August are watering two gardens every other evening, then chopping wood for a week? He won't. He can't. He can't find words for it, for what he knows is happening, what stares him in the face but she won't, or can't, see. The backlash. There was Paris last year in January. And then again in November. Then there was Nice in July. And then the old priest who got his throat slit in his church. And because of all this, he knows it, no one will give him a job.

But for fuck's sake, what's all this got to do with him?

He can't go on like this, howling in the morning to greet the day, walking up to the fork and checking to see if Denis's flag is up. And he can't tell Yolande that's all he does. She'll say something sweet and silly. 'Things'll brighten up in spring,' she'll say. But at the same time, he can't not tell her. He can't stand with her at the window gazing at a robin preening on the terrace banister, their hips touching, his hand on the small of her back, and pretend he's unwinding after a hard day's work.

Perhaps he should. Try at least, try to tell her, try to explain. But he'd have to start somewhere, go back in time, long before Paris last year. Back to that time at school perhaps, when boys he'd never spoken to hated him so much they wanted him gone. And he cried himself to sleep for weeks before he caught one cheating, thanks to a tiny mirror stuck inside an old make-up case his mum had given him. Those he fixes all around the house? He puts them up to see what's coming, to be prepared and try to dodge the blows, the crazy hatred.

But damn it, he didn't see any of this coming, this backlash, here, in the purple-blue mountains where nothing blocks the view. And where life, or so he thought, could never be tilted this way and that by quakes, deep, silent quakes.

She'll come back tonight, beaming, radiant. She'll pull off her cowboy boots, throw them in a corner, settle on the sofa, demand a drink, hold out an arm towards him. He can't go through with it. She might be back with the suggestion of a country dance show for Christmas to raise money for the Nice victims. He couldn't face it. He can't face her. He should go perhaps, just for a while, a short while, a few days perhaps.

Beyond the terrace, across the field, the shadows of the naked poplar trees along the stream are lengthening, ink black in the golden twilight. Coyote stifles a woof, dark clouds gather and there's a hush, the hush before the first snowfall. He takes a pen and sheet of paper, sits at the table and begins to write, long sentences that fill one side of the page and then the other.

He's never wanted to be with anyone but her, since the moment he met her eyes in the rear-view mirror in his taxi and it left him dizzy, dizzy with happiness… He's so grateful she came with him to these mountains. He loves it here with her. The reason he's leaving has nothing to do with her, he doesn't know how to put it into words. He can't quite understand it himself, what's happening. He can't do a thing about it, he's not sure it can be explained, it's so stupid, so crazy. He's sorry. He'll come back as soon as possible. When it's over, when things are back to normal. She mustn't worry. She's left her blue scarf on the table, he's taking it with him. It smells of vanilla, of her sweet, sweet self…

Cheyenne barks. He looks up. A couple of wrens flutter out of a hedgerow. The others have flown away, the swallows, the swifts, the warblers, they've taken height, gone south. That's what he'll do, same as the migrants, flee out of gunshot, look for gentler climes. He crumples the letter into a ball he stuffs inside his pocket and takes a new sheet.

Yolande,
   The birds have gone south. I'll follow them for a bit.
      I love you.
      Yves

He reads and rereads his letter. Tightens his fist on it, screws it up, shoves it in his pocket and takes another sheet. Slowly, carefully, like a school boy learning, he writes the same few words, but signs 'Ben Choukri (your Yves)'.

Dan Blavet

Dan wouldn't look up. His eyes remained on his desk. He twiddled and dropped his pencil, blushing. His thin fingers went purple and his knuckles white as he grabbed it up and closed his fist on it. He didn't turn to his neighbour, chat, or giggle. He just sat in the third row, slightly to the side, where those who wanted to be forgotten sat.

I started the atrocities I was paid to disclose with a whisper. I raised my voice gradually and the finale I murmured or bellowed, depending on how many eyes glazed as the minutes ticked by. I drew a line down the middle of the blackboard and little figures on either side.

'Each one is a battalion, okay?' I drew a couple of matchsticks under the figures.

'Each one means five hundred people. Including children of course.' And I started the guessing game.

'How many should I draw? How many do you think? Give us an estimate.'

They were past that age when yelling 'a billion' was great fun and knew enough, or so they thought, to rub shoulders with the truth. Hands went up, numbers were mumbled. I shook my head, pursed my lips, rolled my eyes.

'Any more guesses? Come on. Can't anyone do better?' Except for Dan's, all eyes were open wide as I slowly filled the board with little figures and matchsticks underneath. Here were the dead and casualties of one side, soldiers and civilians. There were the dead and casualties of the other in whatever war we'd been studying that week.

Whenever I could get hold of the information, I drew a line across the board and another lot of figures and matchsticks. Then I faced the class, fuming to find Dan looking down, and explained that these numbers never appeared in their textbooks. They were the dead and the casualties according to the other side. The discrepancy between the body counts according to whom and where you asked furrowed their brows. It came as an anticlimax to the certainty of horror.

'But then, how can we know for sure?' one would ask.

'We can't.' This was the worst, not to have sure answers, not to know who or what to believe. It opened up an alarming new world for seventeen-year-olds, that of doubt.

'Oh, and by the way, to these numbers you can add, and without a doubt, fifty thousand soldiers who came back shell-shocked and not always whole, I'm afraid, and who committed suicide within a few years of their return.' This I said in passing, as I concluded on the Vietnam War. I never wrote that number on the blackboard. I didn't want them to develop the fact into a paragraph to show off how well they'd learned their elders' lessons. It may have been one of the only certainties I had to offer but it was pushing it too far. I knew the fascination suicide held for young minds.

But for all my gesturing, all my carefully timed dramatisation, my tiny figures and huge armies, when my eyes fell on Dan, his head was bent as usual, as though too heavy for his frail neck.

The small room down a long corridor where I gave my classes overlooked a street empty except for a few battered curtained vans. In these, ladies, out of countries recently liberated from the shackles of the east, sold their bodies. Standing on the dais, listening to a young voice proclaiming 'that all men are created equal, that they are endowed by their Creator with certain inalienable Rights, that among these are Life, Liberty, and the Pursuit of Happiness,' I glanced at the curtains being drawn and when they opened, at men stepping from the back of the van. Across the street, a walled cemetery drew the border—a border we never crossed—between the city and its northern suburbs. An endless flow of cars and lorries glided east and west on a flyover motorway built over the cemetery and, beyond it, the tall grey buildings of our students' estates faded in the fog. The minute the bell went, we rushed down to that street for smokes. Leaning on the school's dustbins, we hurried to exchange the latest before the next bell. In the last years, more often than not, we parted shouting, 'We can't go on like this.'

Things had gone haywire. Phones were pressing, calls urgent. Alarms went off, sirens wailed and people plugged their ears. Kids, parents and teachers held on to their mobiles as to lifelines. Danger lurked inside each bag, bins disappeared from streets, hidden cameras recorded every move, barbed wire grew around buildings, and more and taller walls were built. I began thinking of taking early retirement and leaving the city.

I settled in a remote mountain village, in a small house with a garden open to fields. It was a world I knew little of, a world of howling winds and surging streams, greedy foxes and wild boars, some said wolves. At night, beyond the shutters, unknown beasts snorted, kicked stones, dug holes. When dried leaves whirled, I thought I heard armies moving in the shadows. I wanted the garden walled. Fred, who prunes trees and builds walls in the village, was at the pile of stones in the early morning when weather permitted. He chose the stones like a jeweller, weighing, dusting, turning each of their facets towards the sun to catch a ray. Once he'd placed a stone on the wall, you'd think it'd been there forever. As the sun fell behind the mountain and the wind turned cold, he'd come in and we'd have a drink or two. And off he'd go, back to the late fifties, to when he was conscripted and shipped to Algeria.

'Twenty-four months,' he'd say over and over. 'Twenty-four months of the bloody carnage.' He couldn't get away from those twenty-four months. To each rendering of the story he added new confusion. I never figured out whether it was just after the first putsch, or just before the second, when he walked out of his barracks into the desert to escape from shooting strangers' chests, stumbling over slit throats and hearing the screams of tortured men at night. He didn't go far. He was caught and locked up for a year.

'You keep quiet about it all, don't you?' he'd say, shaking his head. 'You teachers, and historians, and journalists. Hardly a word. Or you bring it up as 'events'. As if it hadn't been a bloody war.'

When he left, he'd turn at the gate and raise his fist. 'You count and get the bullets ready, I'll prepare the rifles!' I'd raise my fist in answer and, in the dusk gathering around the village slumber, tipsy, the two of us, we softly laughed. He swayed down the lane on the wave of the wind, his shadow lengthening as he floated from the lamppost, his red bandanna darkening, bobbing on the crest, until his white curls drowned below the hedges in his garden. But then the walls were built and we forgot about raising our fists.

I have no radio or television. There comes a time when enough unpredictable events befall you without having to join the media's orchestrated laments. Delaying the full realisation of news allows me to drive my thoughts and emotions, and not be driven, or so I like to believe. But as luck would have it, I heard about the bomb attack the minute the world did.

I was having a drink at Fred's. He's all for news and his television is always on. At eight sharp, he put the sound up, filled my glass, pushed a piece of bread in front of me, pointed his forefinger at a plateful of salami slices, and ordered silence. The box's moon face announced that one Dan Blavet had planted a time bomb under F.L.'s—the ex-prime minister's—car, killing him and a passer-by and wounding four others. At the mention of Dan Blavet, I shot up. I watched the moon face talk for another minute and tapped on Fred's shoulder. His eyes remained glued to the telly as he briefly shook my hand.

Blue shadows were flickering inside the two kitchens up along the lane. They were sitting eating, gaping at the blood on the box, no doubt. In his flight after the device exploded, his accomplice or comrade-in-arms, or whatever they call themselves, was injured and caught, and immediately gave his name away. Dan Blavet. They're common enough names taken separately but not that common put together. Dan Blavet was reported to be twenty-nine. He was on the run, nowhere to be found.

I fumbled my key in the hole, locked the door, and haven't left the house since. I don't want to hear anybody's 'Look at what the world's come to.' I want to be left in peace to delve into the bin of the past. Things are left to rot in there and, after a while, there's no telling one year from the next, one group of kids from another. As the piece of news gropes its way through my confused mind, I lie on my bed rummaging inside the bin, raking up those layers that get weighed under the refuse of the present, trying to revert back to the time when Dan was facing me daily, a dozen—or is it eleven? thirteen?—years ago, in search of clues.

One day keeps coming up to the surface. Dan must have been sixteen or seventeen when he walked into the classroom wearing glasses. I've reeled the scene back and forth half a dozen times and the spotlight invariably falls on his shy, reluctant smile in answer to mine as our eyes met. Ah, I thought, so all this time, he simply lived in a haze. He'll begin to *see* at last and to look up and out at the world. But he did not. His glasses made no difference. He went on turning his pencil around his thumb, sitting in that position of submission to authority and exclusion of the world, head bowed. Perhaps he didn't like what he glimpsed. Perhaps he'd fallen into the habit by then. Perhaps his head was too heavy.

'If you want to hit the sky, fuck a duck and start to fly,' I read on his desk. I knew his handwriting well enough. It mirrored his slight body and shy smile. Like sparrows' feet testing an expanse of fresh snow, his words left a light and apologetic trace on his papers. The thin, timid, wobbly letters, scrawled among the usual guns and penises of all sizes and colours, there for all to see.

I caught him doodling in the corner of the margin of his exercise book two or three times when he should have been pondering the Glorious Revolution, or some other oddity of history. Not often though. Not often enough over a period of two years. Or maybe three. I can't work it out in the muddle of the years that hurry down a dark shaft and gather speed as time goes by. Drawing his little doodles, his tiny noughts and eights as he was however, Dan was still looking down, not out. He simply wouldn't take an escape and I wavered between irritation and puzzlement.

Oh, to be the hell out of here. Oh, Lord, deliver me from the bore of learning, just for today if not for ever, please, oh Lord... I could hear the students' silent prayers when their eyes drifted out of the room. They were looking for something out of life, towards far-flung, fairer, sweeter places, dancing in a breeze perhaps, hearing a wave dying away around their feet, or feeling a hand resting in theirs. There was dissatisfaction with their lot, and a hint of rebellion, to appreciate in their window gazing. If, while their bodies and minds were in turmoil, they did not swim against the tide every now and then, but did everything expected, what kind of adults would they become? Submissive no doubt, passive, compliant. Dan's attitude of apparently contented concentration, body stooped over his desk and eyes downcast, did not befit his tender age. But though I revelled in the dreamers' silent pleas, I played my role as best I could and firmly told them that the tree leaves outside would never get them through their exams.

In my nightly stir of the period's dissolving remnants, an unruly bunch float up. They'd blockaded the school. They'd padlocked the gates with bicycle chains. I can't recall the reason for the blockade, what new government proposal had flared them up again. Another group had climbed over the railings and occupied a gymnasium. The police made night raids to force them out but, the next morning, they were back. There were scuffles and blows outside the school gates, rowdy meetings in cafés, shouts of, 'We can't go on like this. Open the school,' and 'Enough. Let's march on the *Assemblée Nationale.*' At night, some of us got in, sat with them on the mattresses in the gym and told them they were right to be angry, right to rebel, but this would get them nowhere. Old friendships were broken forever between those of us who said we should let them be, they were only growing up, those who claimed we should join them, they had no future, they were right, and those who retorted, 'No they aren't. They're breaking the law. Call the police. Get them out.' But the reasons for it all, the chains, the raids, the blows, the sit-ins, the broken friendships, I just can't summon.

One morning, I managed to squeeze in a dozen of my class through a small door we hardly used on one side of the school. We trooped across the playground. The crowd behind the railings spotted us, booed, shouted

'Traitors, Scabs'. We hurried inside the building. Our steps echoed as we marched down the empty corridors. I unlocked the door of our stuffy room. Breathless and dishevelled, we dropped our bags on our desks, slumped at our places, and they laid their heads on their bags.

Who was there? The girl with rings in her nose and eyebrow. Yes. Laura. Her black hair, all over her bag. Can't recall her face. Who else? Dan. Dan was there. As usual, hunched over his desk in the third row, slightly to the side.

'What do you want to do?' I snapped. I hadn't meant to snap. Nothing stirred around the heaps on the desks. Sirens were wailing in the distance.

'Shall we talk?' I hurled the words at the wall. They fell to the floor.

'Would you like to speak about the situation?' There were slight movements around the heaps, and moans and groans and noooos.

'All right. Fine,' I said.

Damn. What now? I too felt like laying my head on my bag. In the first row a girl—Monique?—rummaged inside her canvas bag, pulled out a textbook and dumped it on my desk.

'There's a poem in here,' she said looking up, faintly smiling. ''Annabel Lee',' she whispered, before she let her head fall back on her bag. I could have kissed the girl. I grabbed the book.

'English book everybody. Page 56. Monique please, you start.' She sat up slowly, shook her head, flicked her hair off her face.

'It was many and many a year ago, / In a kingdom by the sea…'

'Laura, please!' And Laura's voice rose.

'I was a child and *she* was a child / In this kingdom by the sea, / But we loved with a love that was more than love…'

The words flowed and filled the room and, as they seeped through their bodies, their backs straightened and their chests and voices rose. When it was his turn to read, Dan had the last lines. He sat up. 'And so, all the night-tide, I lie down by the side/ Of my darling—my darling—my life and my bride, / In the sepulchre there by the sea, / In her tomb, by the sounding sea.' There was a pattern in those words and rhythm in the soothing lull of the wave-like lines, and meaning, and depth in the resistance of a love that lives on after death. And when the bell went, it sounded like an alarm in the huge empty carcass of the building, but we wouldn't budge.

I've hardly slept or eaten in the last two days. I haul myself from bed, collapse on the couch for a while, and drag myself back to bed. I've left the shutters closed to keep out the sweltering sun. The dusty rays break into white stripes across the room and crawl down the wall as the sun sets. The memory tap, on at full throttle, drifts along tangled, broken, messy scraps in the heat of the day. But at night, the flow carries me straight to the small room where I drew my little figures and matchsticks, watching out for a sparkle of righteous anger in the students' eyes or a crease on their foreheads at the mention of an instance of men's follies. And Dan, shy, frail, pale Dan, forever sitting head hanging low, as though he longed to lay it on the floor.

    I move my feet around my bed to find a fresh spot but the sheets are hot and damp. I shuffle to the kitchen, gulp a glass of water, open the window and push the shutters open. An owl hoots. I search the night. A blackboard fills the window frame, with 'Violence is sometimes justified' written across it in big white capitals. I'd drawn lots and Dan was to defend the motion. He hadn't liked it. He ran after me in the corridor and asked if it could be changed, if he could oppose it. No way he would find arguments for such a crazy statement. He couldn't and no one in his right mind could speak for violence. His reluctance was customary. Gandhi and Martin Luther King were always favourites with teenagers. And yet, I'd never seen a student, let alone Dan, in such a state over a piece of homework. He stammered as he spoke in a high-pitched voice. His eyes were gleaming with fear, his fists clenched, his lips quivering.

'Hey, Dan, don't get so worked up. It's only a debate. Think about the French Resistance or the IRA, for instance,' I said, and left him there. I can't recall his arguments, or if they rejected the motion, or anything about the debate, only the way panic had taken over the whole of him when he was faced with the obligation of speaking for violence. It's the only time I remember him reacting to something. He was the kind of boy whose reports, term in, term out, were filled with 'could-do-betters' because it wouldn't do to write, 'sits there, isn't interested, is wasting his time, won't go far,' or simply, 'dull.' Dan was a dull boy. He never had a thing to ask or say in class. He was the picture of submission, sitting head bowed, twiddling his pencil around his thumb. But Dan Blavet is a terrorist on the run.

I must put an end to my rambling and find out more. But only the local paper can be bought at the café. In my first year in the village, I pored over the events of local life. Artists won first prizes with cloudless skies and poppy fields, boules finalists posed triumphant, hunters shot twenty-two roe deer in a day, and their dogs, or their sons sometimes. I got sick and tired of blue skies and poppy fields, villagers' trophies and dead sons. Now, if I have to drive to town to get aspirin, I buy a decent paper. Must do this. Make sure it's him at least.

The shutters have been closed for nearly three days and the car's parked outside the house. If I go on, neighbours will wonder and come knocking at the door. I open the shutters, step into the early evening light and, slightly dazed, walk to the café. No one's there. I sit at the counter and ask Claude for a glass of wine.

'Been too hot lately, hasn't it?' is all he says, thank God. He serves me and disappears inside the kitchen. There's a folded copy of the local paper on the counter. 'Dan Blavet' is running across the top of the front page. I empty my glass.

'Hey, Claude, get me a refill, will you,' I call across the counter. I swig it before I reach for the paper. Just below the fold, Dan, a thin, shy smile on his lips—a picture that must have been taken in his last year at school—is staring at me through his glasses.

Fourteen years ago, his mother fell ill. She had a contaminated blood transfusion, contracted HIV and three years later, died. F.L. was prime minister when he let this happen, knowing the blood wasn't a hundred per cent safe. Six hundred people died, poisoned by the infected blood. The trial lasted eight years and ended two months ago. A doctor and someone who was something in the Health Ministry were given two-year suspended sentences for gross negligence. But then, the case was dismissed. No one held to account. No one charged with manslaughter. No resignations. Dan's comrade-in-arms, the one who gave Dan's name away, was the son of another victim. But Dan was the mastermind. He's still on the run.

A weight falls upon my shoulders, roots me to the counter. I hadn't known a thing about his mother's illness during the years he faced me daily. Would it have made any difference? Instead of 'could do better', I might have written, 'serious and attentive, will make progress' on his school reports. I took his silence for dullness. But what was there for him to say? He never let his eyes wander off towards the sky. What was there for him to dream about outside? Dan's head, hanging low, *was* too heavy for him.

He was stammering and shaking all over when he

was made to argue that sometimes, using violence was right, a moral obligation, the last resort and only option left when all else fails. Did he recall those arguments while he was planning the attack? Did they grow on the soil of his raw and intimate knowledge of despair, death and injustice? Could it be that while he wasn't looking, he was listening, that thoughts were scurrying across his mind and that some of the things we'd tried to teach had been understood this way? Could it be that the tiny figures and matchsticks I drew had left a trace, a trace of anger that swelled into rage, and led to this?

There's a point in a child's life when he stops asking, 'Did I exist before being me? Why am I me and not you?' That's when he becomes a teenager. In his early teens, he moves on to, 'Why do we let children die of hunger? Why can't we stop wars?' In his late teens, he stops asking those questions too. That's when they landed in my class, when they'd forgotten the bigger picture, wouldn't, couldn't see it any more. I believed we were meant to bring them back to it, make them plant themselves in it, work on it and find ways to alter it and make it better. But we're mere word-bags. Damn, the only picture I delivered, week after week, year after year, was of a past that always repeats itself. The dead of one side. The dead of the other side. And the leaders, smug, left in peace.

I uproot from the counter. 'In the sepulchre there by the sea, / In her tomb, by the sounding sea', the last lines of the poem, the ones he read while the city outside was roaring with rage, ring in my ears. I walk down to where the men play pétanque, along the row of cypress trees.

'Just the one we were waiting for! Pick up those boules, will you, and be our third,' a man calls out. Fred's there. He winks. I bow my head. Three golden boules are glittering at my feet. I pick them up, test their weight, roll them in the palms of my burning hands. I hit one against the other, join my feet, bend, throw one. It rolls smoothly and touches the jack. The men cheer. I bow my head, pick up the third boule and send the second rolling. It brushes the first. They cheer louder. Fred comes up and whispers, 'Did a proper job, didn't he, that Dan Blavet? Don't see why those bastards should always get away with it. Hope he does, though.' I nod and bow my head. What I nod at, I'm unsure.

A group of children brandishing pieces of wood come running down the lane, screaming, their faces glowing. Bang bang, they shout, aiming their sticks at us. Bang bang, they yell, firing at magpies and at a cat that scoots up a cypress and catches a magpie. A few bloodstained white feathers softly land at our feet. We win the game. I put my name down for tomorrow's round. It's the semi-finals on Saturday.

Muse

Look at it in the window, that umbrella pine tree, with its deep purple trunk soaring up to the sky across the canvas, slightly leaning under the weight of its boughs. Its boughs, falling back over the other side of the bay in the background, look how their dark green and cobalt blue set off the silver of the shimmering sea below. And the two sailing boats, they're off, off to Sicily perhaps, two butterflies over the wavelets, their wings lined with gold, fluttering in the sky, the sky, merging into the sea, the two blending. And those floating fluffs of downy clouds. Oh, it's lovely, lovely. She cranes her neck, peers inside. That tall dark blue tree over there, on the wall on the right, a cypress? She shades her eyes, presses her hand against the window. At the foot of the tree, there's a long orange shape that looks so soft, so warm. What is it? Oh, how she'd like to take a peep inside, just a peep.

But she's off to the grocer's and the butcher's and then to the wine shop. Imogen's coming over tonight and she'll want her usual bottle of claret when she sits for her meal. And as always, she will be alert to shortcomings, her eye to a speck of dust on the chest of drawers, her palate to a dash of pepper too heavy, a pinch of salt too light, and only too pleased to point them out. Not a minute to waste. Oh, but why not take a quick look inside? The gallery's still closed. She'll go in on her way back. She'll pop in after the wine shop, that's what she'll do.

After weeks of raw cold and wind, a touch of

spring prickles the cheeks. The few people out at this early hour are well wrapped against the still crisp air, it's early March after all. But the buds are out, tiny, but out all right. In front, two schoolboys swing their satchels and break into a run and, for a minute, she hurries behind them.

It's so quiet inside the gallery; it could be empty. But there's someone sitting in the dark at the back. She doesn't know which way to turn. Her eyes, twitchy, edgy, hop right and left from one picture—oh, the sumptuous hues of red and pink—to another, the myriads of blues and greens, they make your head spin. She takes a step to the right, drawn to that tall cypress tree, to the blue-green flames of its branches swirling up to the sky, straining against the gale bringing in whirling dark grey clouds. Her eyes follow the strong dark strokes down the trunk to reach that soft orange shape. A young woman in an apricot dress is lying there, on a slab of rock by a lake.

But wait a minute, wait a minute. What's this? What *is* this? That dress, the colour of apricots, she's seen it somewhere. The raised knee. The green slipper by the foot. One arm tucked under the head, the other resting on the stomach. She's seen them somewhere. But this is preposterous, preposterous. It's her. *She*'s lying on that slab of rock.

She breaks into a sweat, puts her shopping bag on the floor, moves closer to the painting. She must take this slowly, slowly. Start with the background, keep the young woman on the slab of rock for last. She looks up to the top of the cypress and across the canvas to a range of hazy blue hills, lets her eyes follow a path downhill and rest on, what, a cliff? A castle by the lake? But the brush strokes are so light it could evaporate, its pink walls dissolve into the mist lifting from the lake in the breeze. A folly? Perhaps a dream. Her eyes slip back to the foreground and to the slab of rock. It's her. It's her all right.

Someone's walking towards her. She starts, turns, doesn't know where she is for a second.

'Oh. Good morning. I'll come back later,' she mutters.

She shudders in the cold, takes a few steps one way, turns around, walks back, sees a bench, collapses on it. She needs to gather her wits. She stands, rushes back home, drops her bags on the kitchen table, runs to her bedroom, climbs on the stool and reaches for the shoeboxes on the shelf.

Ah, it could be in this one. It's marked 'Italy, summer 1983'. It could also be in 'Spain, Easter 1986'. She takes both down. She hasn't opened any of them since she moved, ten years ago. Just a waste of time looking at old photographs. Look at this guy, grinning. She had a serious crush on him at the swimming pool. Can't even remember his name. This black-and-white merry bunch, who on earth are they? All gone, by the looks of it; the neat perms, the whiskers, the pre-war clothes. Gone, gone, whoever they were. And this gang of giggling schoolgirls, with Imogen and her standing in blue and pink frocks in the middle, they certainly haven't made it to the Other Place yet, but look at them now. Perfect illustrations of the ruthless work of time passing by and the general collapse of things—cheeks, breasts, shoulders. But what a mess. They shouldn't be in this box, these jolly ghosts.

Here it is, in 'Italy, summer 1983'. That vast, dark hotel room—in Capri, was it? No, Naples. God, it was stifling hot in there, though the shutters were half-closed all day. Flies were buzzing all around and the blades of the fan, spinning overhead, made wavelets on her dress, silky, the colour of ripe apricots. She'd dozed on the sofa. That's when he took it, while she was having a little siesta. But aren't her eyes open in the painting? There's the green slipper, by her foot. Her raised knee is leaning against the back of the sofa. Did they get up to anything on that sofa?

She lets her eyes drift from the photo and up at the grey sky outside the window. Thinking of it, she was never much more than a picture for him. Always looking at her through his lens, he was. 'Bring your hair over your shoulder,' he'd say. 'Don't grin, just smile.' 'Turn your head.' 'Look away.' And sitting on the warm wet sand of an Italian beach, she'd bring her hair over her shoulder. And leaning against a balustrade, she'd stop grinning and just smile, and turn her head and look away as he snapped and snapped.

When he walked out after twenty-two years, she was devastated. Twenty-two years. Nearly a lifetime. Her lifetime. Nothing much in the way of fun with men after he left, let's face it. But soon, as if she'd stepped out of a tightly laced corset, oh, how gentle and easy breathing felt. No, he never wanted her as she was, ravenous in the morning and yawning at night, laughing her belly laugh and spitting pips, whistling at the sink or singing one of those old hits she loved. Sometimes, but only if no one was around, he didn't mind her whispering 'You Give me Fever' in his ear, or grabbing his hand and sweeping him off to rock and to roll on 'I'm Just a Gigolo'. He even enjoyed it. But mostly, he wanted her ethereal, a Botticelli, a virgin of sorts, one that would be ready for it any time he was, smiling, with her hair over her shoulder. No way could she slip her hand inside his fly when *she* felt like it. Oh, no.

But how had she made it all the way from the sofa in that dark room in Naples thirty years ago, to a rock by a cypress, on the shore of the Lago di Como or something like it, hanging on the wall of a gallery in this small town? She'll go back this afternoon with the photo, try to work things out. There may be a crowd then, elegant people sauntering along, gazing. They'll stop in front of the cypress as dazzled as she was in the morning and, when they see the young woman resting on her rock, they'll turn around, glance her way and whisper, 'Oh, look, this young woman in the orange dress, look, she's here, it's her.' 'Oh, yes, so it is. So she's the Muse.'

As she starts putting the photos back inside the box, an idea slowly makes its way to the forefront of her thoughts. Perhaps, yes, perhaps she could enquire about the price. And if it doesn't cost a fortune, well, why not after all, she could buy it, couldn't she? She could own it, keep it forever, this picture of herself—young and desirable. She's never bought a painting and it does seem a little extravagant. But it would be such a pity not to buy it—a real shame, a crime really. It would be letting a part of her past vanish. It would be abandoning a piece of herself on the wayside. Yes, if she buys it she'll be rescuing a young woman in full bloom from oblivion, from nothingness, keeping her alive. Never mind if it costs a fortune, never mind. She must buy it. Oh, Imogen's face tonight when she sees it. 'Good heavens, Carol! What's this? It wasn't here last time I came. I say, doesn't the woman look a bit like you? Actually, Carol, she looks a lot like you. Where on earth did you get it from? The woman looks quite lascivious!' 'It's me, Imogen. It's me,' she'll say. And after a moment of silence, she'll add, slowly, slowly, 'I was a model for artists, Imogen. Didn't you know?'

It's called 'The Siesta'. They only managed these afternoon naps during the three trips they took on the continent. And he'd call her 'my lady of the afternoons' on those rare occasions. As if she'd eloped with him. They were husband and wife for heaven's sake. Not that she minded having a siesta in those strange dark rooms, far from it, but an occasional one at home on a Sunday afternoon would have done no harm, would it? They were stolen time, those siestas; time snatched from itself. But to call her his lady of the afternoons. Preposterous. Carried away by his own words. Turning her into his creature with his words. Creating his own world and forcing his idea of her inside it. And blind and deaf to that of others.

The artist's name is Alissa Brown. She hadn't noticed the name was written on the slab of rock just below her feet. The woman didn't get her nose quite right, made it bigger. And her arms, slender in those days, she made plump. And her lips are turned up into a sketch of a smile. Not a hint of a smile on the photo. She was asleep.

It's £400. Her, amid all this, this riot of colours, these hazy blue hills reflected in the lake, this pink suggestion of a castle, these whirling clouds and cypress branches swaying in the wind, a mere £400. 'The exhibition ends tonight,' she hears the young man sitting in the dark tell someone.

She steps outside feeling dizzy. The exhibition ends tonight, he said. No more dilly-dallying. She'll buy it. Not a minute to waste. She rushes home to fetch her cheque book and start the steak and kidney pie. No, no time for a pie, it'll have to be steaks tonight. She begins to remove the bits and pieces from the chest of drawers, the vases, the china, the clock. And then she takes them all down, the 1930s poster of a ferry crossing the Channel, the small-framed prints and watercolours, until the wall is bare. A little out of breath, she opens the bottle of claret, pours a glass and sits where Imogen will be sitting tonight, opposite the wall. Oh, she can't wait to see it there and to follow the soft rays of sunshine piercing the grey clouds, dappling the drapes of her apricot dress, tickling her feet and warming her arms, her neck, her breasts. How new and bright and exciting the room will look. She'll invite people for dinner: her cousins, her old school friends, the young man from the gallery. 'Yes,' she'll tell them. 'It's me. I was an artists' model.'

Just before she steps inside the gallery, she glances at the deep purple pine tree in the window and can't hold back a smile. It's quiet inside, but a woman is standing there, dressed in white, about her age, no, probably younger. There's a blank on the wall on the right where 'The Siesta' was. The woman walks up to her with a big smile.

'I'm Alissa Brown.'

'The picture here, that was here, 'The Siesta', where…' She waves briefly towards the empty wall, unsure what to say, how to put this. Where is it? Where is she? Where did you get her photo from? That's what she wants to ask. The young woman that was lying there on a slab of rock, under a cypress tree, in her silky apricot dress, where did you find her photo? In a dustbin? On a garbage heap? Did you find it in a skip? Did someone give it to you? Who? Where has she gone, the young woman in the painting? Where is she? Why is she not here anymore? She feels a lump swell in her throat.

'Ah! You liked 'The Siesta', did you?'

'Who… where… where did you get the inspiration from?' She hears the quivering in her voice, its faintness, and the stupidity of her question. She wants to run, run away from here.

'The inspiration?' The woman throws her head back and laughs. 'Oh, from a snapshot my partner gave me. He thought it was a rather good photograph he'd taken of a girl, an old flame, I believe. The cypress I copied more or less from a Van Gogh and the background from a Leonardo. That's what art is about, isn't it? Freedom. Freedom to put things together that are not normally seen together, creating new worlds. The girl asleep in that photo, I transformed her into an odalisque, fleshy, awake, alive. I must have made her quite alluring. It was sold earlier this afternoon. The man lusted for her, took her away immediately, eloped with her.' She laughs. 'Glad you liked it. It's been nice talking to you.'

She walks back home in the dusk. She tidies the sitting room until everything is back in place, just as it was. At last, in the gathering darkness, she sits opposite the wall as the room grows colder.

The doorbell rings.

It's Me

It's me.

Yes, made it. Just about. Train's packed.

No, I wasn't late or anything but had the fright of my life.

The-fright-of-my-life.

What? Oh, hang on. We're going through a tunnel. You there?

No, I didn't hang up. Told you. We were going through a tunnel. A tu-nnel.

Don't know. Damn, another tunnel.

Haven't the faintest. Crawling through a town. Marseilles could it be? It's 12. Could be Marseilles I guess. Cor. Everything looks so filthy and derelict.

No. Told you already. I wasn't late or anything. It was Toby. Gone. Vanished. Couldn't find him anywhere. And Monsieur… what's his name, was due to come at 9, get us to Vanessa's and then me to the station.

Oh, Alan, don't you remember? Toby's staying with Vanessa. Anyway. He'd been having a bit of a go at the beauty next door lately.

No. Not Monsieur Thingemmy. Toby. Holding his vigil, watching the beauty-next-door's every move. You know, the sly one with those lovely green eyes.

No. Not the Durands'. The other ones. To our right. Can't remember their name. Dupond is it? Anyway. I was out of my mind. Rushed over to the Duponds' something or other, but when Madame opened the door, there was the beauty, half asleep on the radiator in the hall, sly as ever. T'was obvious neither had seen Toby. Hey, we're slowing down. Blow. We've stopped. We're in the middle of a forest. We're not supposed to stop anywhere. It's a non-stop to Paris.

Did they? When?

No. How long for?

Christ. They're always doing that in this country, aren't they? It's one after the other. Don't they have anything better to do?

Look, that's not what I'm saying. Of course they've got the right to strike. But they do seem to make the most of their right, don't they? Ha. Train's getting the hiccups. Hurray. We're picking up speed again.

What?

Green beans? What are you doing cooking beans at this time of the day?

All right then. Okay. Call you back in ten minutes.

Okey-dokey. Twenty then.

It's me. Look, I'll soon be running out of battery so next time, you call me, okay? I'm in the bar.

Course there's a bar. What do you think? Bet the beans are all mishy mashy.

All right, all right. I was only joking.

What?

What do you mean? I'm thirsty for one thing and this woman sitting next to me seems to disapprove of our conversation. Keeps sighing and rolling her eyes and shooting me dark looks.

Exactly. And I told her to go get a life. She didn't seem to get it.

Wait a sec. I'm getting there. So he wasn't in the house, wasn't in the garden, wasn't after the beauty next door and Monsieur Thingemmy was about to arrive. Can you imagine the state I was in? Everything ready. The old blanket you'd cut up for him in his basket.

No. Brownish.

Yes, that's the one. And his pills.

Oh, Alan. For his rashes.

Yes. His rashes. Have you forgotten about his rashes? You do forget things easily, don't you? Can you imagine him itching and scratching and bleeding while he's at Vanessa's? It's going to be a whole week after all. Poor thing. Anyway. I was getting frantic. Damn. They're slowing down again. What's wrong with this train? Where are we for heaven's sake?

The sea? Oh, dead right. Just there on my left. Still not heading north then, are we. Alan, you there? Alan, is there someone with you?

Well, I thought I heard footsteps in the background. Hang on. Did you hear this? Look, they've just said something. Couldn't get it. I'll call you back, okay? No, you call me. I'm running out of battery. I'll try to find out what's happening. Give me half an hour, okay?

What do you mean just like that? They were saying something. And I'm on my mobile, aren't I? And if I run out of battery, I'm finished, aren't I? Where am I supposed to plug it in? You took your time calling back anyway. At least an hour, I'd say.

Yeah, still in here. It's crammed. A couple of kids are screaming and running around like headless chicks. Train speeded for about fifteen minutes, hiccupped and stopped again. Hasn't moved an inch for nearly an hour. The barman's getting worked up cos they all want food and water and all he's got left is beer and plonk. I asked him what the matter was. He doesn't speak a word of English. A barman! On a train! Thank god I speak some French. Anyway. He said something about *un mouvement social*. A movement! Social or not social, not exactly what I'd call a movement when we've been at a standstill for more than an hour. Anyway, that's all I could get from him. He sounded relieved I didn't want any water.

No, plonk. What do you think? This is France after all, innit? And only five quid a bottle.

Look, I'm trying to tell you. If only you didn't interrupt all the time. Now you know the woman from across the street.

Yes, reddish rather.

No, not skinny, come on, nice and slender. Well I was rushing around calling To-by, To-by and she appeared on her doorstep and said she'd heard someone had found a horribly wounded black cat earlier this morning and had rushed it to the vet's. The state I was in. Damn. They've just said something again.

Look, Alan, I can't speak very much louder than this. The ticket man's just appeared and he's having an argument with a young bloke. People are getting loud. The bloke seems to be saying he wants to be reimbursed. And there's this other guy shouting something about hostages. Yes, he's saying we're being taken hostages. Damn right he is. That's exactly it. We're being taken hostages.

What do you mean be careful? What do you want me to do? Jump off the train and walk all the way to good old Blighty? Thing is, it's getting stifling hot in here. I guess the air conditioning system is out of order or something.

No. Impossible. We can't. Not on this kind of train.

Look, this isn't the pre-privatisation Flying Scotsman or Golden Arrow.

Don't be daft. Of course we can see through them. I'm just saying we can't open them. No handle or anything.

Yeah, okay, if you like, but a cattle wagon with windows. If you didn't always insist on flying, you'd know. Anyway, it's just like the Eurostar come to think of it. Oh, Alan, I'll never get the connection to the Eurostar if this goes on. See if they say anything on the telly about this mess. Look, there's too much noise in here. Call me back in a bit.

Oh, it's you. Hang on. This woman's leaving. Cor. No bigger than a bread plate.

The seat. I can barely place half a buttock on it.

Cos the aisle's blocked, crammed with bags and kids. Couldn't get through if I tried. Well at least I'm sitting. Things are a little quieter now. But we're still not moving. Alan, what's this? I can hear those footsteps again. Where are you? Are you in the living room? Who's there? Who's there with you?

All right, all right. But it did sound like footsteps.

Yes, okay, okay. Where was I? Yes, the vet. I rang him. Thank God he spoke a little English. His description didn't quite fit Toby's. Black with white paws, he said.

Well, no, not exactly. Only two of his are white.

Oh, come on. I know for Christ's sake. You never look at the poor thing.

Well, can't say you take much notice of him. Anyway. Couldn't bear to hear what the vet had to say. He'd broken a leg and lost an ear.

What do you mean his four? Only the front ones are white.

Oh, the back ones now? Do me a favour.

Okay, could be the back ones I guess. Can you hear me? Christ. The ticket man's back. He's trying to make his way along the aisle. An angry couple have grabbed hold of him, wanting to know how much longer we'll be stuck here without an explanation and an apology and information on what's going to become of us. Everybody's getting worked up again. It's four o'clock. We should be arriving in gay Paree. I'll definitely miss my connection to the Eurostar. Alan, please listen to the news and tell me what the hell is happening here.

Haven't a clue. Somewhere between the Med and the Channel. In the middle of nowhere. In the middle of a yellow field actually. Been stuck in this blinking field for three hours now. Not a soul in sight, not a house, no village, nothing. Black clouds are rolling in the sky. There's a line of cypress trees across the field all bent to one side. Wind's blowing like hell. Train's swaying. Oh, Alan. I can't bear it anymore.

How on earth would I know if there are any vines? What difference would it make anyway?

Pussy fussy? What are you talking about?

Pouilly Fuissé. Ha ha ha. You've got a nerve joking, considering.

Yeah. I'll try to get back to my seat. Bum's all sore anyway sitting on this saucer. You call me back.

Okey-doke. Give me half an hour. I'll stop at the loo on my way.

What do you mean an hour? Switched the thing off to save the battery. Where am I supposed to plug it in? Tried three loos. Won't describe the state they're in. No water in two of them. Water, but sink blocked in the third. No loo paper. And the stink! When I think I paid for a first class seat and have to put up with all this worse than third class mess.

Yeah, back at my seat. It's getting cold and dark. Blusters of wind are rocking the train. I'm exhausted, Alan. And hungry. Won't make it to London tonight, that's for sure. Won't even make it to Paris.

Yes, okay, the Toby story. Poor thing. After the phone call to the vet, I...

What do you mean you've had enough details? I'll remember that, Alan. You've never really cared for him. I know it.

Look, let's not argue about this. But you must admit I'm the one who feeds him and plays with him and cuddles him and talks to him.

Okay, okay. Yes, he got back all right. Barged inside the kitchen mewing like his head had been wrung off. I managed to grab hold of him and put him in his basket just as Mr Thingemmy was hooting and we zoomed down to Vanessa's and then to the station to catch this bloody train. Alan, who's that?

That person. That person who's with you. I can hear her. Walking. Who is it, Alan? Answer me, Alan. You there? Damn. Battery's flat. I'll try and get it refuelled. Call back!

It's me. Managed to plug the thing in. It's completely dark Alan, and a group of men in overalls and with headlamps are walking along the railway track, banging their tools on the train, just below the windows. It's awful, Alan, really scary. They're going to take us hostages. We're going to spend the night in here. No water. No food. No heating. Nothing. Have you listened to the news? Have they said anything?

Nothing? Not a word? You mean hundreds of people are stranded in the middle of France and nothing is said about it? Have you tried the radio?

Dramatising? What do you mean? I'd like to see you in this shit. What do you think they're doing walking along the train with tools? It's serious, Alan, don't you see? They're going to keep us locked up on this train till they get god knows what, fewer hours I suppose and better pay and extra holidays.

No, come on, I'm not being unfair. I'm not responsible for whatever situation they're in. Why should I pay for it and be treated this way?

All right, all right, let's not argue about this. But listen, Alan, don't hang up, please, let's talk for a bit, I mean really talk. We never have the time, do we, or never take the time. Or rather, you never have the time. First of all, Alan, please, tell me why you always want to fly back to England? I mean what's the real reason. And why did it have to be three days ahead of me this time? Why? And please don't come up with the need to air the flat and do some shopping again. Why do you never want us to leave together? What's the real reason?

Yes, Alan, there is someone shouting. But please, for Christ's sake, don't find excuses not to answer my question.

Yes, it's this man across the aisle having a fit. He's banging on the window, shouting at them to open the door.

Yes, yes, the train is making strange noises. God, it's starting, crawling along, speeding a little. Shit, it's slowing down again, stopping. We're at a station. Can't read the name. They've opened the door and letting people on. They're crazy. The bloody train's full, packed full and a group of people with heavy luggage are getting on. The man across the aisle is shouting, asking them to close the door again. Hang on, Alan, they're making an announcement.

It's me. Can you believe this? The mess isn't due to them, but to that fucking social fucking movement. They said these people's train was cancelled and they've been waiting at the station for three hours and would we be so kind as to share our seats. The cheek they have. No one's giving up their seat. It's turning into a huge row. Oh, Alan, it's freezing cold and I'm hungry and knackered, and I'm not giving up my seat.

Sleep! Oh, for Christ's sake, Alan. Is that all you can come up with? Your tired old way out of any situation you can't cope with. Go to sleep and things'll sort themselves out somehow. It's a jungle in here, Alan. People are fighting for space, for water, for food, and you're telling me to have a nap. Men are keeping us locked up and you suggest a lie down. Hey, train's starting, picking up speed.

What? Speak up, we're going through a tunnel. A tu-nnel. Can't hear you. Don't hang up.

Alan, you there? Please tell me, why did you want to leave before me? Why? Did you want to get away from me? Why aren't you on this bloody train with me. Tell me. Why can't we ever talk? Alan, you there? Alan. It's me. Phone's dead. Oh Alan.

Last Time

'Last time I'm doing this,' he says.

They've been driving a hundred miles and there's still over three hundred to go. Or rather, he's been driving. She never drives on the motorway and in the sleet, only in summer, when he lets her, on small winding roads, with her window rolled down and her elbow resting on the ledge. Last time he's doing this! He says it every single time they travel up to her hometown in Northumberland, when they're about half way. But they're not past Bristol yet and out it comes. She gives a little shrug he doesn't see. After weeks of what do we do?, where do we go for Christmas?, they always end up driving North. But not last year. She couldn't make it last year. She had a broken rib.

The thick, wet fog hasn't stirred since they left this morning. If the red figures on the dashboard didn't flick ahead, you'd think time had stopped. They haven't exchanged a sentence since they started, just bare words to assure survival.

'Crisp?'
'Mm.'
'Water?'
'No.'
'Petrol.'
'Okay.'
'Pee?'
'Yeah.'

They stop for petrol, pee and coffee after Bristol and as they trudge back to the car in the slush and fading trails of the shops' flashing green and blue lights, the cold seizes her. It rushes in when they get into the car and moves along her limbs as he shifts gears with quick sharp movements of the hand.

He used to squeeze her knee before getting into first gear. The first time he reached for it in the dark and the slightly sickening smell of crisps and tobacco, she closed her eyes as though she were sliding between warm sheets with her tummy full. The sensation quickly turned into a feeling she couldn't articulate. I've never been happier was what she told herself when the car gathered speed and whizzed past all the other vehicles. Nothing can really matter from now on. Dying would be all right.

She'd been sitting with her girl friends in the pub and couldn't take her eyes off the man playing weird, bumpy-paced music on the piano in a pool of light in a corner of the room.

'I'd go anywhere with a guy like that,' she said, lapping up his dark hair falling over his forehead, his long thin fingers running up and down the keyboard, his shoulders moving at one with those erratic tunes that led you gently to one place and then jostled and rushed you to another.

'Yeah,' the friends said, 'let's buy him a drink when he's finished.'

After he'd downed his beer, he winked at her. 'How about a breath of fresh air?'

He tore off past the sleepy town's darkened windows and she felt pulled away from the world she knew, high above it. With sweat gushing from every pore and heartbeat wild, she felt awake, real, alive like she'd never been. And then on, whenever he zoomed down bends at eighty miles an hour missing trees, skimming ditches, stopping short of parapets on bridges, the thought came that life could end now, now it had coursed right to the core of her. Squeezing her knee in the dark one minute and tossing up her life—and his—the next, he was wiping away days, months, years of hazy longings while gazing out of the window at dreary skies over grey narrow roofs, thinking her life was wasted.

Except for the purring engine, the car is silent. Birmingham's lights flicker faintly on the left. On the right, a dirty orange glow hovers above Nottingham. The fog's lifting and the tarmac's dry. Shoulders tense, knuckles white on the steering wheel, he revs the engine and presses the accelerator. Not a soul on the road. Just two long, sharp beams piercing the night, stiff dark shadows, naked trees or poles, rumpled snowdrifts on the bends, a dim light or two in the distance. They could be the only ones left in the whole country, the world come to a standstill. She closes her eyes, her head lolls, and she dozes off.

She was just nodding off the night he raced down a sharp bend in sheets of rain and she had grabbed and pulled the door handle of the old Ford Cortina. It was their first car with seat belts and she hadn't wanted to be strapped in, but he'd forced her. The wind blustered, the door scraped the side of the road and fell, torn off its hinges. He stomped the brakes. The car skidded and stopped dead. He turned the engine off and they had sat, shaking, the roar of the motorway flyover above their heads and the rain splashing in, soaking her. He punched the steering wheel.

    'You could have killed yourself,' he bellowed. 'If it wasn't for that fucking belt, you'd be dead, lying on the road, run over. And what would be left then, hey? What? You tell me.'

What would be left of what? she'd wondered. Of her? Or of him? Of him left without her? Or of him having killed her? But then, he wouldn't have been blamed, when she'd refused to fasten her seat belt, when she'd dozed off and opened the door by mistake. They would have said he'd done his best to protect her. They would have pitied him and he'd have got away with it. He gets away with murder.

Half asleep, she lets that old what if…? unfurl once more. What if she'd died that day? What if she'd been injured and paralysed? She spends more and more time weighing things, trying to work out if what was (he saved her life that day) and what is (she's still here, sitting next to him) is better or worse than what could have been. But answers never come clear cut, thoughts get tangled, and she gives up.

Her head falls on her chest. She starts, opens her eyes. The beams are hazy. They must be past Newcastle. The mist turns to fog, thickens, shrouds them. There could soon be patches of ice. As he knows but he isn't slowing. And she sees it, hopping out of the hedge, ready to cross the road, its tail erect, its round eyes shining in the headlights. She grabs his arm, shouts, 'Stop!' A dull thud. He jerks out of her grasp and shoots along. She turns away from him, slides down her seat, limp as a rag doll and stares at the door handle. What if…? What if she does it, unfastens her belt, throws open the door and joins the tiny bird?

'You killed it,' she mutters.

'Don't be a fool.'

As if testing the power of the engine he speeds along for the last few miles of the motorway, changes gears with angry gestures for the exit, swings right onto the road. He's going to say it again. He always does at some point after turning onto this road. But *she*'d like to say it now. Last time I'm doing this. She'd like to say it before he does.

He turns left into the lane. The car screeches to a stop.

'Last time I'm doing this.' Ha. Later than usual.

'The torch. Where is it?'

'How should I know? *You* packed it.'

'The keys?'

'In your bag. Don't you remember?' He pulls the suitcases out of the boot. She gropes under the seats, picking up wrappings, gloves, bags. He sweeps aside a cobweb in the door frame, kicks one suitcase then the other along the corridor into the living-room. She follows, loaded with a rucksack hooked over her shoulder, bags in both hands, a loaf of bread under her arm. She trips over a suitcase. The bags and the bread fall to the floor. She unhooks the rucksack from her shoulder, drops it on the bread. He turns around, glares.

'What do you think you're doing?'

'Doing? As usual. Nothing, nothing at all. Unloading, actually.' She blows into her hands, stamps her feet, hops around the bags.

'Dancing, are you? In anticipation of a lovely Christmas, I suppose?'

She sticks her hands in the pockets of her long, navy coat and faces him. He looks grey standing in the harsh light, with the dark shaft of the corridor leading to the stairs behind. His jaw line's getting fleshy. He's balding. There are bags under his eyes. He's tired. Still. That tiny bird—a thrush? A tit? A wren? It happened to be in his way and he killed it, and then zoomed off as if to celebrate.

'I'm not dancing. I'm hopping. I'm cold. And it was *your* decision, as always, to come up here at this time of the year.'

'Oh, for shit's sake,' he shouts, kicking at a suitcase. His grey eyes narrow, gleam, turn black. 'Can't you change the tune now and then?'

Here it comes. It's been a while but here it comes, his good old wild, rough, feral self, the one he keeps just for her, when no one is around. Shouting, swearing, kicking.

This is what being alive is about, she'd told herself when she moved in with him and it started. Kicking at chairs standing in his way. Swearing, but with the windows up, at drivers he found too slow. Yelling if the eggs broke as she slid them onto his plate.

For months he'd picked her up from her home at dusk and driven along the edge of the moors till it was time for him to play at the pub. He'd drive her back after closing time and, breathless and frustrated, they'd sit in the dark below the dimly lit window of her parents' bedroom. He'd cup his hands over her breasts and she'd push them away then pull them back again, press them against her lips and gnaw at his fingers. 'We can't stay in this hole. They sleepwalk through their lives. Let's go south,' he said.

And on her twentieth birthday he whisked her off. She threw a suitcase in the boot of his car, glanced at the two faces behind net curtains, screwed up with worry, waved briefly in their direction, slid down into her seat and closed her eyes. He squeezed her knee hard and she felt it surging deeper than ever, that warm flow inside her stomach and all along her limbs. He shot off and, as he moved to the fast lane of the motorway, she turned towards him and watched his clenched jaws pulse, his nostrils flare, his thigh muscles swell. He was racing her down the country to the town in Devon where he'd found a job. As fields and towns flashed by, she was sailing on the crest of a wave, shedding her past, leaving her drab life at long last.

And after a year, she had her little bruises. At nightfall, after he left for the hotel where he played his jazz tunes in the bar till the early hours of the morning, she'd sit at the kitchen table and pat them gently. As if her skin were his, she'd softly press her cheek, her lips and tongue on those she could reach, on the inside of her wrists, on the top of her shoulders. They were his little gifts. They prickled and stung and throbbed all day so that not a second passed when she was without him. They were his presence in the night while he was gone, a reminder of what she meant to him. They were his love bites.

She's cold. She stamps, blows into her fingers. He clenches his jaw and fists, lifts a bag and sends it flying down the corridor. She stops and squats. The bull's out in the ring. No waving of a red flag. Play it gentle. Give him something. Keep him in check. She opens the rucksack, digs out a woollen hat, lifts her hand up in his direction, but keeps her head low. He takes a few heavy steps towards her, grabs the hat and pulls it over his head. Keep him sweet.

'I try to keep him sweet,' she told her friends. She gave them snatches of her life over a drink after her pottery and yoga classes, snatches she slightly altered. 'Sometimes,' she said, 'I want to leave.'

'Why on earth would you want to leave? Some relationships work that way,' said Betty, after a yoga class. Betty's husband, with whom she never had an argument, went to get some petrol one morning and was never seen again. Staring at her empty glass, she frowned and added, 'And they're the ones that last.'

'Perhaps. But I told him the other night. I told him I might leave one day,' she said. 'And after he'd yelled, 'No, you won't', he drew the curtain so hard, the rail fell, and he stormed out slamming the door, not even noticing he'd left with the curtain over his shoulders.' She chuckled and they laughed.

'Batman! Never a dull moment in your life, is there? That's what you get when you live with an artist. Stop moaning, you lucky thing,' sighed Jane, whose husband asked for his bath to be run at 6.45 p.m. every day, pulled his chair up to the table for his dinner at 7.15, watched TV till 10.30 and then went to bed.

'I'd call the RSPCA if only a tenth of what he does to you, he did to my Toby,' exclaimed Sally, whose only companion was her cat. 'But come on, nobody's perfect. At least there's a man in your bed at night,' she added, her blue gaze lost in the mist outside.

The night he slammed the door as Batman, she hadn't said she might leave. She hadn't said a thing. She'd left. She'd been arranging coats and jackets in the hall, but she was in his way. The blow came hard, as if a knife had sliced her arm. She gasped and bent over. He left without a word. As the sound of the engine faded in the night, she heard her heart beat loud and couldn't catch her breath. She grabbed her coat, stepped outside and wandered in the streets. She found herself on the road to Bristol and entered a small hotel where her voice came out faint when she asked for a room. She lay on the bed with her coat on and her eyes open, listening to the cars. The cold gripped her as the hours went by. And the same thoughts and questions kept turning over. Why hadn't she waited till he left? She'd had time to hang up the coats in the hall. Why hadn't she given it a thought? If only she'd given it a little thought, she wouldn't have been there, in his way. And over and over, she pictured his every move from the moment he stepped into the house till he pushed the bedroom door open. She couldn't go further.

She thought her chest would burst when she imagined him standing in the dark, empty room. She walked back home at dawn, dazed and shaking. He had yelled, he had drawn the curtain so hard the rail had fallen, he had slammed the door. But what she didn't tell her friends was that after shouting, 'How could you do this to me?', he'd slapped her face so hard she fell, and locked the door behind him and only let her out the next day.

'He won't let you go because he's still in love with you. Madly. And after all those years,' said Maureen after a pottery class, hugging herself. Maureen's partners came and went, never staying more than a few weeks at a time.

She was right. He was still in love with her, when his muscles tensed and his eyes gleamed. He was madly in love, when he stood there, towering, ready for it, a yell, a blow, a kick. He loved her to madness when he smashed a plate on the wall, a glass on the floor, when he bit, burned, slapped. Only she could bring that out in him. And when he buried his face in her neck and whispered, 'I'm sorry, sorry, I didn't mean to, don't ever leave me, I need you,' and then, when he showered her with soft things, a bunch of flowers, a pair of gloves, a scarf she showed off to her friends, she knew she'd not done everything she could to keep him sweet.

But she never revealed her little bruises. At first she drew over the scars with marker pens. The cigarette burn on her wrist she turned into the clasp of a bracelet made of small pink roses. A stem followed a vein up the inside of her forearm with wild liana, swarming with bees and moths and music notes twisted around it. A lotus flower unfurled in the bend of her elbow and the stem grew around her arm up to her shoulder where, covering other scars, it burst into red lilies. And over the soft round top of her shoulder, a couple of blue butterflies with dots and lines on their wings was poised to fly on the petal of a lily in full bloom. To keep them there forever she had them etched into her skin. When she pulled up her sleeve, her friends gasped at the strange beauty of the scene. For just round the corner, inside their friend's house, so close to their dull, grim lives, a mysterious, shady yet exciting existence, that was the stuff of films, was unravelling for real. Perhaps she wasn't going through life unscathed but she wasn't half alive, like them. When it was time to part, rolling their cool, empty glasses over their hot flushed cheeks, they said, 'And anyway, where would you go if you left? What would you do? Join our girls-at-the-till brigade? Come on.' And that's exactly what he always said: you're better off at home.

'You used to like coming here at this time of the year.' The woollen hat has done the trick. His voice has softened. He's trying to play a tune on her, pulling out his nostalgia score, the one he knows used to draw tears from her. They've long run dry but she'll go with him, tune in for as many extra bars as she can, in the hope that the shadows on his face start lifting, his eyes go back to grey, his fists relax.

'Yes, and we jumped into bed, didn't we, and stayed there till the walls warmed up. Two days sometimes.' She smiles in his direction but not at him, his cheeks tonight, grey and sagging, a deterrent to reminiscence.

'And we don't anymore, is that it?' His voice is rising, his male pride pricked. He's interpreting, thinking there's reproach. But there is none. He's out of time. Try again. Try tuning in again.

'No. No. It's just that it was... wonderful when we did.'

She feels drained, crouched over the rucksack under the harsh light. She's exhausted, striving, day after day, year after year, to stick to his score. She sits on the floor, extends a leg, upsets a golden paper bag and a cracker rolls out to his feet, glimmering. He picks it up and shakes it in her direction.

'How about pulling a cracker?' He expects her to tilt her head on the spot and smile, to jump to her feet and run to him, to pull the cracker and for another few days, weeks, with a bit of luck, life goes on.

Life went on. She stopped going to her classes. She'd learned over the years. To always be there, on the lookout for a change of mood. When best to play along, when to keep her mouth shut. To always wear a scarf, or gloves, or a necklace he'd bought her. To check and double check that ashtrays, cushions, glasses were exactly where he wanted them. To serve him perfect eggs. And quivers sneaking in on her lips and on her fingers didn't give her a boost anymore but came as warning signs. Stop, danger zone, run out of sight and out of reach. Since the blow in the hall and the night at the hotel, followed by the day and night locked up in the bedroom, she had an icy stone weighing on her stomach. She felt a lump in her throat, so big at times she couldn't swallow. Her heart went wild for no good reason and there were days she could hardly breathe. She'd taken to stealing outside after he'd left for work. With the rain and the wind whipping and slapping her face, she staggered across the fields and over the hill behind the house, until exhaustion took over and smothered the fear she'd walked in all day long. Then she lay on her side of the bed and waited.

But he'd come back early one winter night and found her gone again. He was sitting in the dark, naked on the bed, when she pushed the door open. He sprang up, grabbed her by the shoulders, threw her on the bed, climbed on top of her, tore her knickers off, crushed his knees against her hips and held her by her wrists. He pinned her down and tried to thrust himself inside her. She screamed and kicked and bit and clawed and writhed till just below her breast, a rib went crack. She gasped and stiffened and he rolled off. 'You did it to yourself,' he said.

The wound was far too deep for her to press her lips upon and there was nothing on her skin that could be turned into a flower. As she could barely walk, and even breathing hurt, she stayed indoors. After months of slow, small steps and shallow breathing, it healed. And winter came. And they sat in the car this morning and drove up to her hometown for Christmas.

After long hours with the seat belt around her chest, the pain comes awake. She's worn out, freezing, starving. She lifts the rucksack, grabs the crushed loaf, pulls out a slice and nibbles.

'Hey, look here.' He points the cracker at her. 'We didn't have to come here. I suggested going to a hotel for a change. To France, Italy, the fucking North Pole. 'A hotel? Whatever for?' That's what you replied, didn't you? *You* did not suggest anything. You never do. Look at you, squatting like a little girl, blaming it on me when you never suggest or do a thing.'

They're sneaking back on her lips and fingers, the little tremors. She can't play his score anymore, can't tune in. But he'll kick if she remains silent. Say something. Quick.

'It was the South Pole you suggested, not the North.'

'Oh, it's the North Pole you wanted to go to, is it? Oh, I'm sorry. I really am. I should have known.'

He kicks at a suitcase, comes to her, sniggering, shaking the cracker in her face. She holds her breath. He pulls both ends. It goes pop and a plastic car falls out. He throws the pieces of cracker at her, picks up the suitcase—it's his—storms out, leaving the front door open. She wolfs down the piece of bread. The car door slams. The engine starts. She presses her fists against her mouth, stares at the front door, turns her head, following the sound of the car down the lane. It reaches the main road, picks up speed, roars, tears the night, and fades away.

She springs up, steps on the toy car, grinds her boot on it. Face contorted, fists clenched, she shrieks and crushes it, kicks and stamps. She runs to the door, slams it, locks it. Panting, she slumps down to the floor. She puts her arms around her knees, presses them gently against her chest. She lays her cheek on her knees and closes her eyes.

First time, she whispers. First time he's ever done this. Leaving. Taking his stuff and leaving. Leaving her. Leaving her alone. In her house. First time she's back home, alone in her own house. She'll stay. Yes, she'll stay in the house where she grew up. She'll be safe here, at home, alone. It's so quiet and peaceful. It's getting warmer. She'll go up to her bedroom in a minute. She'll take her time up the squeaky stairs. She'll open her bedroom door, walk to the window and draw the soft blue curtain against the wide black sky. She'll undress and slide between the soap-smelling sheets on her narrow bed. And soon, she'll be sleeping like a baby, dead to the world. Yes, she'll go up to her room in a minute.

A car is racing up the road, roaring, tearing the night, turning into the lane, screeching to a halt in front of the house. The engine stops. A door slams.

John's Your Man

It starts early in the morning now. At first only a slight contraction, as if a hand tensed on my stomach, but then it's sneaking up inside me, extending its fingers, gripping the whole of my chest. I stay motionless, gazing at the square of dim grey light behind the flimsy curtains on my right. There's a lamppost just outside the window and you'd think it's dawn all night, a bleak November dawn. But now, I know when the sun's up. The hand's there. Until last month, it lay low and didn't start moving its creepy little fingers till I got home at night. But now, it's here all day.

Thing is, Pete was around until last month. And you can't just drop the box or the chair you're carrying and say to your employee, look mate, face it, things aren't looking good and aren't likely to get any better and I didn't sleep a wink thinking about it. You do what's to be done when you're a boss. You can't afford to whine about the worries that keep you awake half the night. You shove them deep inside and nail a lid on top. Contemplating your navel and disclosing what you see there is the last thing you've time for when you're in my position.

So me and Pete, we wrapped and packed and piled and carried people's beds, tables and carpets down narrow staircases, and loaded the van. And we zoomed up and down the roads of Suffolk and unloaded, unpacked, pulled out and carried people's belongings up another lot of staircases. When we saw some of the stuff people wanted to pack and transport to their new homes, he'd wink. There'd be dozens of dirty Styrofoam cups, or old shoeboxes crammed with rusty zips and broken buttons, or big plastic bags bursting with small plastic bags. A posh old lady, she had dozens of paper bags filled with chunks of stale bread inside the wardrobe in her bedroom.

'For the ducks,' she snapped when she caught us raising our eyebrows.

One guy's kitchen cupboard we found full of women's wigs, red, black and blond, curly and straight, short and long. 'Hey,' Pete whispered. I looked up from a box. He was swaying his hips with a blond wig and a big diamond necklace he must have snatched from a drawer in the bedroom.

Pete was a bit of a teaser and we never talked much, but I reckon we saw eye to eye about our trade. Whether dirty cups or rusty zips, bits of bread or funny wigs, we packed them with as much care as we did the china. It's none of your business the way people lead their lives, is it? On our way back, I'd whistle to the radio tunes and he'd join in, slapping his thighs. Popping a crisp inside his mouth, he'd quack, 'For the ducks,' in a high-pitched voice and posh accent. If it wasn't too late on a Friday night, we'd stop for a game of darts and I'd buy him a pint or two at the Hounds.

John's Your Man Removals was in high demand from the start. Phone rang first thing in the morning and was packed with messages when I got back at night. The order book and ledger got filled in at full tilt. 'John's my man,' girls giggled. 'John's our man,' mums declared. Pete, who I'd hired for only three days a week to begin, quickly worked full time. He got a mobile as soon as they appeared on the market, helped deal with customers, gave me the thumbs up after a call. Business was thriving. Until about six months ago.

In September I think it was, I took my order book

out on a Sunday afternoon like I always do to check what was ahead for the week to come. It said something like, Monday morning, delivery of cardboard boxes for Mrs. Tilbury. She's doing the packing. Removal for old Mr. Smith in the afternoon. Shouldn't take more than a couple of hours. Poor bloke doesn't have much and is only moving down the road. Mrs. Mellor on Tuesday morning. Now she's a hoarder. It'll take the whole day. Moving to the other side of Ipswich and unloading on Wednesday morning. Loading and moving for Mrs. Tilbury on Friday morning, thirty-eight miles down to Stowmarket. And that was it. Trifles on the Monday, nowt on the Wednesday afternoon, nowt on the Thursday, nowt on the Friday afternoon, and not an estimate in sight. That Sunday afternoon is when I felt it for the first time. A punch straight to the stomach. I took a look at September the year before. I had twice as many orders and more than a few quotes lined up. And another punch straight to the stomach. My breathing speeded and I started panting like I was running the London marathon.

The hand grabs me earlier each morning and I'm trapped. Sweat's pouring down my spine one minute and I've got shivers the next. Heart's battering at my chest. But I'm in my bed, for Christ's sake. Come on, I tell myself, could be worse. There's no hand on your stomach, no fingers squeezing your lungs, no chain fastened round your neck. You've got a roof over your head and a few mates to have a good time with now and again. And then there's Jane, a lovely girl I've been dating a couple of years and… Well, that's it. My business, my 'baby', as Jane calls it, the business I created from scratch, my own little company, John's Your Man Removals, going down the drain.

I kept putting off telling Pete. He has a three-year-old and another on the way. Like I said, we never talked a lot but that much I knew. I never let on how bad things were. I told Jane business wasn't what it used to be and I might not be able to keep Pete full time forever, but couldn't get round to telling him. She said she'd seen him driving the latest Ford Montego, music blaring out the windows and a pretty girl sitting next to him, and that I'd fall ill if I didn't stop fretting over things. Jane's a secretary and hasn't the faintest what it's like being on the deciding side.

You can't just blurt it out, can you? Can't tell a man to his face, you're fired mate, and leave it at that. Some things need wrapping up, words that'll smooth things down. For weeks I racked my brain to find those words that wouldn't hurt his feelings but would make him see it was nothing personal. Driving back home after I'd dropped him at the stop where he caught his bus, I tried all sorts, checked the sound of them, their weight, wondered how best they could be put together.

For starters, I dithered between, 'It's been a great five years,' and, 'You're a great one to work with.' He'd guess immediately it was over with the first one but the second would soften the blow, so I decided to say both and go on with, 'I reckon we've been a really good team you and me.' He'd like to hear I saw us as a team. And I wanted him to know I was grateful he'd never let me down on those wet and freezing early mornings and late nights. I turned the idea round and round and in the end, thought I'd say it straight, just like it was. 'I really appreciate you never letting me down on those early mornings and late nights.' Wasn't sure about telling him I couldn't have done it without him. True enough but aloud, it sounded like a lot. 'I wish we could have gone on that way,' was the best I could think of to bring the tough part up. I'd add that the whole thing was a shame at some point, 'cos, damn, it was a real shame. A couple of words perhaps on dwindling orders and the economy you couldn't fight. And then, eventually, the dreaded finale, 'I'm sorry, Pete. I really am. I can't employ you anymore.'

But that Friday night, we were sitting at the Hounds

downing our pints and I don't know what came over me. The credit on the van was out first and then, one after the other, the things I had on my mind just tumbled out, neither here nor there, all in a dreadful muddle. The bank loan for the van and the monthly payments, the new covers to buy, the economic crisis all over the papers and on the telly every night, the hand squeezing my stomach, the orders falling, the price of property rising and people staying put, no one asking for an estimate, the future looking bleak, the sleepless nights, the price of petrol and cardboard boxes, even the price of bubble wrap.

'Oh, shut up, will you. Spare me your details,' is all he said. He was white as a sheet. He grabbed his jacket on the back of his chair and clumped out of the pub. I hadn't uttered a single word I wanted him to hear, not one of those I'd said out loud over and over. I swear I hadn't wanted us to part that way. We didn't even shake. He'd left half of his pint and after I knocked mine back, I finished his and ordered another and then I can't tell how many others. I'd meant to give him a month's notice so as he could sort himself out but he wasn't there on Monday morning and I haven't seen him since. Until yesterday.

I haven't been in touch with Jane for a bit. Haven't called her. Haven't returned her calls. But she'd left a message in the morning. 'I'm coming over tonight,' it said. I'd heard that tone before and knew it meant: whether you like it or not. You'd better pull yourself together, I thought, go and get something for when she's here. I was just coming out of Tesco's loaded with bread and eggs, peanuts and a bottle of wine and he was sitting waiting at the traffic lights in a brand new peacock-blue van, looking ahead, whistling, tapping on the steering wheel. And when the van started moving, I saw it unfold. *PETE YOUR GENTLEMAN MOVER*, in big, fancy, white lettering running all along the side of the van. There was his mobile number underneath. It took a minute or two to sink in, and pang, a punch to the stomach. And the hand was creeping back, tightening its fingers around my chest. I went weak at the knees and my heart raced out of control. Somehow I got back home and sat in the dark, shaking and gasping. When the doorbell rang and rang, I didn't budge. You can't invite a girl in when you're shaking like you've got Parkinson's now, can you?

It must have started when he got that damn mobile, keeping the customers for himself. And me, blaming the economy! But I don't know. I swear he was white as a ghost when he stood and left that night at the Hounds. Can't believe he was putting on an act.

When I haul myself from my bed, it's past eleven. Nothing much to carry around these days apart from myself, so there's no need to hurry, is there? I put the kettle on, lean against the sink and I'm knackered. Just up and knackered already. I gaze out the window and wonder how I'm going to get through the day ahead. The van's parked just outside the window. It's got a flat tyre. John's Your Man Removals is covered up with graffiti and you can hardly read my phone number, or his, just underneath. Couldn't hold my mug straight this morning and it slipped from my hands. Couldn't be bothered to mop the tea or pick the bits. Just went back to bed and stared at the square of dim grey light behind the flimsy curtains on my right.

At the Bottom of the Garden

'Reeady, steeady, goo!' 'I'll let go when we get to the pine tree, come on girl,' the father shouted. 'One, two, three, goo!' Over and over.

Summer was ending and they were still at it, father and daughter, round and round the garden, every single afternoon. When, a little out of breath, the father said, 'Let's have a break,' the girl dropped the bike, ran to the nearest bush, crouched to find a grasshopper or a beetle to tickle, or stood on tip toes to watch a spider weave its web. After a bit, the bell sounded, signalling cycling practice was about to resume. She buried her head deeper inside the leaves for a minute or two till more impatient, it sounded again. And on and on, round and round the garden, the father running behind, hand on the girl's shoulder or on the rack. 'Now, girl, go on, pedal, pedal.'

She wasn't one to run to her mother, cry in her bosom and beg for mercy, or one to rebel, stamp her foot and say, enough. And anyway, what could she complain about during those long afternoons when the sole object of her father's attention was her? Wasn't happiness just this, feeling his hand on her shoulder as he ran behind her? So just as they reached the pine tree and he gave the bike a little push and shouted, 'Now,' the girl dropped her feet firmly on the ground or flung both legs high up into the air to make sure the next day he'd be there, for another of their very own merry-go-rounds, round and round the garden until dusk crept in and they heard the mother shout, 'Enough you two. In you come. Double quick.' It allowed no delay and the father gave the girl a gentle slap on the back, pushing her towards the cottage. Ravenous, she scampered off. He followed slowly, carrying the bicycle on his shoulder.

Days were growing shorter. One afternoon, just before they got to the pine tree, without a word, the father sauntered off to a corner of the garden the girl had never been to. She dropped the bike at the foot of the pine and followed. They reached a small clearing hidden from the cottage by a eucalyptus tree and laurel bushes. The father sat on the stump of an old tree, let his hands hang between his knees and stared at the ground. The girl sat at his feet and watched the ants scurrying in line along dry blades of grass holding breadcrumbs twice their size between their front legs. She picked a twig and scraped the dry earth around the insects in the hope they'd drop their burden and turn wild. But they skirted round the twig and got back in line, undaunted. Why did they always walk in line? It was maddening to see such tiny beasts so serious. Where were they going? Where did they live? How did they manage to carry such big loads? She was about to voice the dozen questions rushing through her mind when she glanced up at her father. He was still looking down. She bent to find what could be grabbing his attention on the ground, but not a tremor there. He was staring at nothing, or at something she couldn't see.

Darkness began to spread. The shadows of the eucalyptus branches lengthened, reached her father's ankles and her legs, and released a scent so pungent it made her head spin. Dusk was closing in on them, the din of the world receding and fading. She felt as if they were stranded on an island shrinking as the dark, heavy tide was rising. She shuddered and made a tiny move to be closer to her father, but in the stillness, didn't dare disturb his strange aloofness.

'In you come!' The call tore the silence. The girl

froze. Like two crooks now, knowing the slightest noise and tiniest movement would reveal their whereabouts and be the end of them, they didn't budge. After another, 'Come on in you two,' the father slowly unfolded his body, looked at the girl and smiled a new, funny little smile that didn't reach his eyes. He ruffled her hair, picked up the bike and placed it on his shoulder. 'I guess we'd better go,' he said. The girl didn't shoot back to the cottage. In the secrecy of those moments, she'd stepped into a foreign land and had grown taller and older so fast, she wasn't sure who she was and how to move anymore. She tried to match her father's stride—two big steps to one of his, no, one big step, one hop, no, two hops, one small step, she tried them all—and side by side, they walked back to the cottage.

At the kitchen table that night, the father looked somber and weary. The girl thought that perhaps he was tired of running round the garden in the afternoon and disappointed with her cycling progress. But then, he was the one who straight after tea, bellowed, 'Time for cycling practice.' And he never seemed angry when she flung her legs up in the air or dropped them to the ground. Maybe he wasn't happy with the way she treated the bike. It had been his present for her seventh birthday, a present she hadn't asked for and thought a little scary. No one she knew rode a bike in the streets of London and she hoped she would never have to. But it was a present from her father, and when it had appeared at the front door, she'd thanked him.

The next day, as she was expecting his little push on the shoulder at the pine tree and none came, she placed her feet on the ground and turned around. He was taking the path behind the laurel bushes again. She wheeled the bike behind him and when they got to the clearing, he sat on the stump and stared down at his feet, hands between his knees. She stood in front of him and inspected the saddle, pulling it up, pushing it down. No reaction. She turned the handlebars right and left and tightened her fists around the brakes. He paid no attention. She squatted by the pedals and made them spin and spin around her finger. Nothing. She stood and sounded the bell. 'Why are you sounding the bell?' he asked without looking up. She shrugged, lay the bike on the ground, sat at his feet, grabbed a twig and resumed trying to get the ants to drop their burdens, scatter and have a bit of fun. But as cheerless as her father had become, they remained in line. After a while, even before they'd heard the mother's call, the father stood, stuck his new, funny little smile on his lips, ruffled her hair, picked up the bike and pushed her gently on the shoulder to walk in front of him. She spotted a yellow and black butterfly on a white laurel flower, gave a little shriek and held out her hand to touch its wing. The father grabbed her arm, pulled it back and hissed, 'Don't,' as sudden and strong as a slap on the face.

'Why?' she shot back. He tightened his fist around her arm.

'Don't touch it.'

'But why?' There was a sob in her voice.

He released his grip around the girl's arm. 'Because it's frail and beautiful.'

'But I just want to touch it, that's all.'

He let go of her arm and looked at her without his funny smile.

'If you brush the dust from off its wings, it won't be able to fly anymore. And it may die.' He turned and started walking fast. With a load of a hundred questions and feelings impossible to formulate heavy on her chest, she followed, kicking stones, punching trunks, tearing leaves off branches and letting fat tears roll down her cheeks. 'In you come, you two,' she heard her mother shout as, ahead, her father stepped inside the cottage.

They were leaving in two days' time. By the end of the morning, clouds rolled in and turned dark. Soon after lunch, thunder roared and rain came down in sheets. They stood at the kitchen window, the three of them, and watched the path that ran around the house swell into a foaming, muddy river.

'Will there be frogs and snails in the garden tonight?' the daughter asked.

'Yes,' the mother said, 'and toads.'

'And alligators?'

'Yes, there might well be.'

'And crocodiles?'

'Yes, crocodiles too,' the mother said putting her arm round her daughter's shoulders. The girl looked up at her father on her other side. He was shaking his head.

'No cycling today anyway. We'll do it tomorrow,' he said, giving the girl's hair a little ruffle.

The mother pressed her daughter against her body. The girl looked up at her. She was rolling her eyes and shaking her head.

'I'll start packing,' she said and left the room.

The father went to sit on his stool, started snapping branches on his knee and dropped the pieces into a crate by the fireplace, ready for when they'd come back for Christmas. The girl took an old newspaper from the pile on the floor, rolled its pages into balls she carefully arranged in the fireplace and built a tent on top with twigs and small pieces of wood. She was the vestal of the cottage and knew that the night they arrived, she'd be the one to strike the first match. She trembled with excitement thinking how the paper would curl as she offered it the tiny flame, how it would turn blue, red and orange, swirl and go wild as the fire caught all the balls and twigs. And then, she'd throw in a few pine cones, and bigger branches, and the three of them would sit and watch till their cheeks burnt and the whole room glowed. When all was ready for the winter fire, she stole out of the kitchen and into her bedroom, pulled the bedcover over her head, reached for *The Secret Garden* on the bedside table and for the torch under her pillow, and slipped into her other life, inside a garden that felt more familiar than the one around her with the silent, shadowy clearing she'd caught a glimpse of and walked a few steps in those last couple of days.

In the morning, not a ray pierced the curtains when she woke and the sewers smelt and she felt the sheets sticking to her legs. That meant that once again, clouds would burst around lunchtime and soon, frogs, snails, toads and alligators and crocodiles too perhaps, would roam the garden. And inside her tent, she'd be able to shut out the world and spend another afternoon running wild amid the roses of the secret paper garden.

Finding that dinnertime was a little slow in coming, she crept out from under the bedcover and walked towards the kitchen humming to herself, 'Mistress Isy, quite contrary, how does your garden grow? With frogs, yes loads, and snails and toads and crocodiles all in a row.' She was about to push the door open when she overheard her mother sounding cross.

'Look, let's give this a break.'

'Okay.'

'Why don't we try and do something together tomorrow, the three of us. It's our last day.'

'Okay. What?'

'Well I don't know. We could go for a walk along the coast for instance, and have tea somewhere.'

'No cycling then.'

'Oh, leave her alone. What's the point? She won't ever use the bike in London, will she? And anyway, you don't seem to realise she's still a little girl.'

'And that's the way you want to keep her.'

'What are you talking about? She's too small, that's all.'

'I suppose so.'

The girl rushed back to her bedroom and curled into a ball under the bedcover. He supposed so, did he? But apart from yesterday, when he pulled her back from the butterfly and sounded really angry, not once had he told her off that summer, as he had the previous summers, as a father would if he thought his daughter was just a little girl. And what about those long moments when they sat, still and silent as darkness fell in their hideaway behind the laurel bushes, in defiance of the mother's orders? 'I suppose so,' uttered, surely, only to please her mother. The phrase buzzed round and round her mind like a stupid fly. Oh, how she hated it, the push she felt towards this foreign land her parents lived in. There wasn't much talk at the dinner table that night and on her mother's face, she caught a trace of satisfaction she didn't like at all.

The next morning, a ray of light ran across her bed and woke her up as it touched her pillow. She drew the curtains. The garden was shining. She opened the window. It smelt of wet grass. She heard clanking in the kitchen and hammering in the shed. She tiptoed out of her room. Left untouched for a week now, the bicycle was leaning against the wall in the corridor. She took it down the front door step and onto the path. She sat on the saddle, placed her right foot on the right pedal and pushed it down, then she placed her left foot on the left pedal and pushed it down, and right, left, right, left, her feet pushed and pushed. And the wind blew under her nightie and in her hair, and her hair flew around her face, and soft dewy leaves stroked her forehead, and droplets of water fell on her naked knees and shoulders, and she whizzed past the kitchen and past the shed, and she zoomed past the pine tree and the laurels, and a frog leaped out of her way, and she told the snails, hurry, hurry and the grasshoppers, higher, higher, and the mother shouted, stop, stop and the father, slow down, press the brakes, and she pedalled and pedalled, faster and faster, and flew down a path till it petered out in a jungle of hawthorns and brambles and dog roses and thrown off the bike, she landed on a pile of prickles and looked up at the sky and lay there, arms and legs scratched, triumphant, alone at the bottom of the garden.

When Christmas came, there was no mention of travelling south to the cottage. The girl often pictured the bike, leaning against the wall, abandoned in the corridor, and the stool in front of the cold fireplace with the crumpled paper and the pine cones, and the pieces of wood in the crate on the floor in the dark kitchen. The picture was suffused with the strange gloom that had fallen with the dusk that evening in the clearing. She guessed it was born long before then and felt it hovering at home now. She would have liked to ask about why they stayed in London for Christmas, why the cottage was never mentioned, why the sadness, why it was impossible to ask. It had something to do with words. They were like birds. You know what they're up to in a cage but let them free, and one will go and perch itself up on the highest branch of the tallest tree in the garden, another will fly east and the third west. Yes, words were as unpredictable as birds. And unreliable. Out of your mouth with one meaning, into someone's ear with another. When she managed to get to the end of a question she strived to formulate in her bed at night, more often than not, it sounded silly and useless in the morning. Even her father and her mother were short of words for anything that really meant anything. Perhaps important things simply could not be turned into words. Anyway, when you did succeed in asking a question out loud, if an answer came, more often than not, you wished you'd kept quiet. So the girl didn't ask why they never went back to the cottage.

After Christmas, the father left and went to live in a tiny flat. On Saturday mornings, the girl would stand at the window and when the old car appeared round the corner she ran down the stairs and on Sunday nights, as soon as they were past the corner, she looked up at the window and saw her mother's shadow behind the curtain.

In the last week of April, the mother and the daughter moved to a small flat south of the river. On their first Sunday, they took a bus to a bridge and the mother said, 'Your dad will be waiting for you on the other side.'

The girl spotted him, tiny across the bridge. 'Don't run,' the mother said.

She walked slowly, then faster, then she ran, but just a little, when she saw the smile on her father's face went right up to his eyes. He was holding the bicycle. They walked to a nearby park and she sat on the saddle and right left, right left, she pushed on the pedals and rode like the wind along the paths, swishing past her father, never losing sight of him sitting on a bench, reading a newspaper. In the evening, the father and the daughter walked back to the bridge, the daughter wheeling the bike.

When they got there, she sat on the saddle and the father said, 'Now, girl, go on, pedal, pedal!' and they laughed and she pedalled faster and faster across the bridge. She slowed a little when she made out the frown on her mother's face. The girl looked back and waved at her father. The next Sunday, mother and daughter walked to the bridge, the daughter wheeling the bike, and they saw the father's tiny silhouette on the other side.

The girl sat on the saddle and the mother gave her a gentle push on the shoulder and said, 'Go on, girl, pedal, pedal, but not too fast!'

When the girl reached the other side of the bridge, the father threw both arms up in the air and waved at the mother, and the mother waved back.

And to and fro across the bridge every Sunday throughout the summer and the autumn till winter came and the bike, too small now for the girl, was left somewhere in an attic. The dark kitchen and the cold fireplace, the dusky clearing and the ants and the butterfly on the white laurel, the dew on her face and the grasshoppers, the bed of brambles and thorns and the sky above flitted in and out of the girl's mind and dwindled and slowly went down the shaft of time till they settled at the bottom of her memory, and joined the bike there.

The Footstool and the Suitcase

The day I arrived for the summer months at my grandparents' home in Provence, my grandmother would make me stand straight against the window frame in the living-room. She'd lick the point of a pencil, draw a line above my head, write the date underneath, comment on the space between the lines, and lament my catching up with her.

Despite her shrinking and my growing since the previous summer, we'd quickly put our routine back in place. As my granddad bustled about in the kitchen and the smell of olive oil, thyme and garlic tickled our noses, I'd sit on her footstool in the glow of a morning ray, place my arms on her lap and pull the skin on the back of her hands. I modelled it into hills and plains around the blue rivers of her veins whose course ran above the white and brown ridges of her bones. When it was her turn to pinch the back of my hands, we moaned to see it remain as flat and colourless as a desert.

After lunch, I joined her for her siesta behind the closed shutters of her bedroom and begged to be told a story. My favourite, the story of the barley sugar stick man, was short. But it was so amazing I asked for it again and again in the hope she might add new details and it would last till it was time to fling the shutters open.

'What did he do, Granny? What did he do?'

'*Bou diou*. I've told you a hundred times. He told little girls that if they followed him, they could lick his barley sugar stick.'

'Did they follow him, Granny? Did they?'

'Some did. The strumpets. The silly, naughty ones.'

'Where did he take them?'

'Inside a deep, dark forest.'

'And? And?'

'They fell inside a hole they couldn't come out of.'

'Did they ever get to lick the stick, Granny?'

'No one knows.'

'Why? What happened to them?'

'No one knows. They were never seen again. Now let me sleep.'

I let my grandmother close her eyes for a minute.

'Granny? What were they like, these little girls?'

'Just like you,' she whispered, 'just like you.'

'But I'm not a trumpet. What about the man? What was he like, that man?'

'Like most men.'

I couldn't get over it. Deep inside a forest, at the mercy of a strange man who was like most men, little girls fell inside a hole, were trapped, and never seen again. All for a taste of sweet barley sugar. I shuddered, squeaked and hid under the sheet, but at the same time, I felt so snug on the tiny island of my granny's bed, the safest place on earth, and so proud to be privy to such incredible happenings.

'Please, tell it again,' I pleaded.

'What?' she sighed.

'The story. The one about the man with his barley sugar stick.'

'I can't remember it. Stop fidgeting.'

'Of course you can. He talked to little girls on their way home from school and waved his stick about and promised them they could lick it if they followed him.'

'Oh. Where to?'

'Oh, come on, Granny. A forest.'

'A forest?'

'Yes, you know. A deep dark forest with all sorts of huge trees. Oaks and pines and beech and eucalyptus. And wild animals.'

'Oh. And did they?'

'What? Follow him, you mean? The little girls? Granny! Only the trumpets did. The silly, naughty ones.'

'And?'

'Can't you remember? They fell in that forest. Inside a hole. They were trapped in it. They couldn't come out. And there were animals inside the hole. Mice and spiders and vipers. And the little girls were never seen again. Perhaps there was a wolf in the forest. Granny, do you think a wolf ate them? Ate the little girls—alive?'

It was exhausting filling in the blanks my grandmother left and feeling so many emotions all at once.

'Now your turn, Granny. Please.'

There came a summer when I'd grown too big to sit on her footstool and she too frail to have me join her for her nap. A few summers later, she didn't get up to draw a line above my head on the window frame. I tiptoed to her bedroom. She lay silent on her bed, staring at the ceiling.

After she died, I went up the dark spiral staircase, opened the door to the living room and walked to the tall window. I stood straight against the frame, placed my hand flat on top of my head, twisted around and saw it was exactly where she'd drawn the last line three years before. I slid down the frame, sat on the cold red tiles and tried to lower myself to the first line, in vain. As I walked down the stairs I thought I heard two dull thuds after each step, and felt as burdened and lonely as if I was carrying the dead bodies of two small persons I had to leave behind to close the front door, and face the daylight. One was very old; the other, a child.

Then the window frame was painted over, and the house sold.

She never did a thing, my father said.

She let my father do it all, the cleaning, cooking, clearing.

She'd tap her forefinger on the table, pointing at a stain. She tapped until my father wiped it clean.

In the morning she'd sit at the window, shutters half-closed and watch who was doing what, who was going where, who with.

After lunch, she lay on her bed and read her pocket romances.

When the sun was down, she'd go and sit on the bench across the street and gossip with her friends.

And when it was hot, she went down again after dinner and sat on another bench for more gossip.

She never had a good word for anyone.

And she'd shout. At my father because he didn't bring in enough money. At her sister, Agathe, because she was always out and about. At me because I was in the way, and needed books.

And she'd throw plates on the floor. Against the kitchen wall. Out of the window, against the back wall of the chapel.

But when I lay on her bed in the semi-darkness of stifling afternoons, my grandmother told me stories no one else did, neither my teachers nor my parents, neither my books nor my friends. As I sat on her footstool pressing against her legs under her soft blue gaze, she let me mould landscapes on the back of her hands and walk two fingers I called Tim and Tom along the ridges of her bones and the rivers of her veins. How on earth did we inhabit the same world, my father and I, live under the same roof, eat at the same table and speak the same language when his mother was nothing like my granny?

'This is where I was a prisoner in the winter of 1943.'

It must be what my father said in the summer of 1963, or perhaps it was 1964, as we stood in the sun, squinting up the round tower of the Fort du Hâ in Bordeaux. He was driving me from London to Spain, the land of his forefathers, and I, learning Spanish at school, couldn't wait to show off my command of the language and be my father's interpreter. I was eager to cross the border and hear Spanish for real. I was sweating, thirsty, craving to be in the shade. I was wearing my first bra under a striped blue mini-dress. My head was full of the Beatles' songs. And for the first time since the war, my father was back at the Fort where he'd been imprisoned. I doubt we exchanged many words. My guess is I didn't say a thing. And he, aware that geared towards the days to come I was reluctant to turn towards the past, must have kept quiet rather than risk catching a glimpse of a stifled yawn. But later that day, as we sipped a glass of Perrier water sitting at a café down by the Garonne River, once again, he told me the story of the suitcase.

My father was twenty-two in 1943. He'd fled his village to avoid the Compulsory Work Service, had joined a Resistance network and taken to the Maquis in the Landes region. They were captured by the Gestapo. Three of them ran, were caught, tied to a tree and shot. The others were imprisoned in the Fort du Hâ. The prisoners were to be deported to Germany. Before deportation, they stayed one or two days in the Gare de l'Est in Paris and were allowed to walk along the platform for a couple of hours. My father went to the railings at the far end of the platform and gave a stranger a letter to give to the only person he knew in Paris, Pierre, a journalist from M., his village. The next day Pierre came to the railings and handed my father his press card. My father didn't go back to the train. He flashed Pierre's card past the guards and ran. Two policemen shot at him, but he raced down the stairs of the metro station and escaped. He remained in hiding under a false identity until the end of the war. He'd left his suitcase with all his belongings on the train.

She went into a rage when I came back to the village after the Liberation and told her I'd left my suitcase on the train, my father said.

She said I should have gone back to get my suitcase.

She told the gossips on the bench she had an ungrateful son, back from Paris empty handed.

She told them I had given away all my belongings, linen, shirts, jumper and good leather suitcase to the Germans.

The pictures that took shape in my mind when I heard the story as a child, and again that evening down by the Garonne, are wedged to every part of me. They still creep in, every now and then, at night, unexpected and unsettling. Even at the close of a quiet clear day, I sometimes find myself running away with a heavy suitcase I can't keep closed. It contains all my possessions and is splitting at the seams and the lock and leather straps are breaking. People are chasing me, their boots resounding on the pavement. A jumper falls out, a book, a batch of letters, my hairbrush. I bend to pick them up and stumble. A shot is fired. I stagger up and run down stairs and up again. I know I will be caught, crushed and trampled if I stop. I lose a shoe, my coat is ripped apart, falls off my shoulders. The suitcase is getting heavier. I'm out of breath, gasping for air. I can't go on. I fall, naked, the battered, broken suitcase empty at my feet.

You do not choose your inheritance, or your nightmares. But if you can throw old cumbersome furniture in a skip, burn letters, shove documents in boxes on the bottom shelf of a cupboard in the attic, you can't reduce your nightmares to ashes or drop them in a bin.

My grandmother's footstool has followed me everywhere. Perhaps her fears too, born in an era ensnared between two world wars, have stalked me to this day. Her husband, the son of a Spanish immigrant, back from the horrors of the trenches, looking for work, settling in her village after he got her pregnant, attempting to create his own business in the early thirties, going bankrupt, unable to pay back the loan for the truck he'd bought; her son, coming home from school one day, finding half the village in front of their home, the furniture piled on the pavement and her, shouting at the bailiff supervising it being loaded on a lorry; being forced to sell most of their land and to ask for separation of property so that their home itself wouldn't be seized; the separation, published in the local newspaper.

My father's flight and near loss of life mingled with my grandmother's losses and fear of losing all they had, crammed in that suitcase, passed on, insistent, and as alive, in the still of my nights, as if they had been mine.

M., 23 February, 1944

My dearest son,

Your aunt Agathe came back from her errands full of her usual gossip. But amid this endless flow of words I barely listen to, something caught my attention. Henri, Pierre's brother, will be going to Paris next week. There are times when she reaps something of importance from her to-ing and fro-ing. At the grocer's yesterday, she met Virginie, who was only too pleased to let her know her son was off to Paris. I've been too tired these last few days to go anywhere so Agathe has been doing our shopping. But as soon as the sun sets, I shall run to Henri's and ask him to take this letter with him. I hope Virginie won't be around, as I don't think I could bear to see that smug smile form on her lips if she finds me asking for a favour. I do hope Henri will find you without too much trouble.

We are so relieved to hear you are in Paris. Your father found cuts of beef for a *daube* and opened a bottle of the 1938 *cuvée de la Tour* for the marinade and Agathe got half a dozen oranges from our cousin Louise's garden. As you can imagine, she didn't give them away easily and Agathe had to beg for them, insisting that her sister was poorly, which is no lie. Your father put the rinds of two oranges in the pot, just the way you like it. It has been on the stove since dawn and I hope the smell hasn't reached the Oliviers downstairs. You know how quick they are to talk. I will bring Henri a few chunks of the shin and the chuck tonight, and we will have the rest, thinking of you.

Although I was besides myself with joy to hear you were in France, I must confess a thousand questions torment me. I cannot help thinking you might have been safer working in one of those factories, here, or even over there. I wake up in the small hours of the morning and cannot go back to sleep imagining what terrible risks you took and wondering how you manage to feed yourself properly. I will ask Henri if he minds taking a piece of goat cheese and a couple of oranges to give you. I am worried sick thinking of you in constant hiding in this weather. My only small comfort comes when I imagine you wearing those shirts I made, one on top of the other perhaps, and the warm jumper your aunt Agathe knitted, on top of them.

Your father thinks some of the vines have frozen. They will have to be pulled out in the spring. And there may be more, as winter is far from being over. We won't have much help for the picking when the time comes, with all our young men gone. The village is so terribly empty.

My dear son, the sun is setting and I must get dressed and run to Henri's. Your father is complaining I've taken up too much space. I shall leave him the rest of the page, not much, that's true. Your aunt Agathe, who's off again, sends her love.

Please look after yourself my darling son and write to us as soon as you can.

Your mother

I have indeed very little place left, but enough to tell you, my dear son, how happy we are to know you are safe, and in our country. You are constantly on our minds.

Your father, who loves you dearly.

She thought nothing of eating meat bought on the black market, my father said.

She thought I could have worked for the Germans, in one of the factories they'd requisitioned in France, or even in Germany.

She thought I could have worked for those my father fought in the First World War, those who left him coughing and howling at night, and wheezing all day long.

I found the letter in a shoebox as I was clearing the garage in which my father had stored documents and furniture after the sale of his parents' house. It is the only record I have of my grandmother's voice addressing her son before I came. Nearly half a century after her death, it rises with the anxious inflexions of a mother whose son, hiding in an unknown city, must be cold and hungry. At odds, once again, with what my father said. Her only small comfort comes, she writes, when she imagines him wearing the shirts she made for him. She had embroidered her son's initials on those shirts, white work, chain stitch. And on his towels, red work, cross stitch. Shirts and towels that were to last a lifetime, left in the suitcase, left on a train, bound for Germany, in 1944.

And before the First World War, the young maiden

she was had embroidered her own initials, red work, back stitch, on dish towels; white work, chain stitch on bed linens, tablecloths, napkins; white work, French knot daisies and leaves on her petticoats and nightgowns. Kilometres of thread unwound to mark what was her only property. Hours and days of sitting by the window bent over the cloth, stitching, in and out, and stitching dreams perhaps, in and out, through her head. Tickytacky dreams born from the romances she read. Dreams reined in, not allowed to go astray beyond the limits of her world, the outskirts of the village. Dreams broken by one world war and then another, giving way to fears and rumours growing as they travelled from one village bench to another, spawning yet more fears and people like the barley sugar stick man, the paedophile serial killer, whose story I never tired of hearing.

There was a framed photo of my grandmother from those pre-wars days on the mantelpiece in the living room. Hair pinned up in an elaborate swirl around her head, elbow negligently resting on a pedestal table, waist held tight in a lacy dress, she gazes in the distance. But in the garage where I found her letter, I stumbled on a photo I'd never seen before, stuck at the bottom of the drawer of my grandparents' kitchen table.

Standing in her friend Virginie's garden with flowers in her plaited hair, my grandmother is wearing puffed-out knickers and a blouse with short puffed-out sleeves. She is holding a glass in one hand and a stick with a star in the other. Head tilted to the side, smiling like a mischievous fairy about to use her magic wand, she is surrounded by my grandfather, her sister Agathe, Virginie, four other men and women standing or kneeling, and three children embracing a big dog with a straw hat. They are laughing, obviously having a jolly time. Next to the group, the first words of the refrain of a popular song of the time, *Le Prisonnier de la tour*, are written in white chalk on the gate: *Si le Roi savait ça Isabelle,*

Isabelle si le Roi savait ça. The date at the back of the photo is 17 October, 1950, six days after my birth. My father must have sent a telegram from London announcing it. And that angry, violent, unfair, lazy, mean, narrow-minded mother, suddenly turned grandmother, had gone off to celebrate, with family and friends, fancy dresses, sparkling wine and songs.

Taking a break from tidying the dark dusty garage, I went for a walk up my usual path in the mountain. On my way down, as always, I watched the big white horse lying in its clearing, head turned towards the path. He stood out against the tender green of the grass in the slanting light of the late afternoon. I'd never been near the horse and on a whim, decided to cut through the scrub to the clearing. As I approached, the horse turned into the profiles of three solemn-looking men gazing up the mountain. When I reached them, I saw three boulders that must have fallen off the rock, rolled down and landed there. Gone were the men, gone the white horse. I continued down across the scrub to get back to the main path, and just before a bend, looked back. The big stones were hardly visible against the massive rocky mountain in the background. By a trick of light, a trick of perspective, a trick of time three shapeless stones, now a tired horse, now the sculpted heads of three proud men, now insignificant pebbles.

As the grey-blue glow outside the window darkens, the day's reality fades and slips away. A moment here, then like a ghost, all gone.

    A footstool. A ray of light.
    A story. Closed shutters.
    The tower of a fort. A prison.
    A glass of water by a river. A suitcase.
    A nightmare.
    A letter.

A photo.

Fragments. Scattered fragments of memories as impossible to grasp as moving clouds, as meaningless as jig-saw pieces fallen from a box. But they're all I'm left with of the past and its many facets. No choice but pick the fragments up, move them around, mix them with dry facts and stitch, fastening more words to them before they go for good. The way I did behind the closed shutters of my granny's bedroom, filling in the blanks she left, and walking Tim and Tom on the back of her hands as I sat on her footstool in the morning light.

Smog

Smog smothered London for weeks back then. Double deckers slid like steamboats in streets that smelt of coal and soot and beer. Along the cold black river, foghorns seemed drowned, as distant as if the ships were already past the estuary. Sky and water merged. In between the two, coughing shadows slithered glistening pavements under yellow-haloed lampposts.

    Fog moved in at school, crept along corridors, stole under desks and chairs, hovered near the ceiling, shrouding the teacher's head at times. Desks, doors, railings, everything we touched was cold and damp. After school, I'd lie on my belly in front of the tiny gas fire in the living room and do my homework with burning cheeks and freezing toes. Outside the window, shapes were fuzzy, colours dim and the church bells hoarse. It was an undefined, elusive world, fluctuating with the wreaths of smoke billowing over roofs. And the language I heard out there was as hazy as that foggy world.

    Inside the classroom however, clarity prevailed. Even on days when teacher and black board were blurred, words stood out. Every object you set an eye on, every sensation, feeling and idea had a word fastened to it, a good long feminine or masculine French word, whose Latin or Greek roots reached so deep it was as solid as a rock. And being long, words were weighty and substantial. Each consonant whip-cracked, each syllable filled your mouth and sent vibrations up your nose and down your throat as you spoke. Words were dependable. Once you'd examined, defined and classified them, you described how they were related and meaning would emerge. Before putting pen to paper, if you asked yourself the proper questions (the auxiliary: to be or to have? the object: before or after? the verb: reflexive or not?) and followed the rules carefully, nothing could go wrong. There was a clear-cut syntax that followed the subtleties of feeling and nuances of thought in French. And no one could resist or fail to be convinced by the clarity, balance and accuracy of its rhetorical devices.

It was the language in which I'd learned to have a grasp on things at home, to tie my shoes, tell time, lay the table, agree, refuse, ask. It was the language my teachers used to disclose the order behind the chaos of the world: the outbreaks of wars and the rhymes of poems, the currents of oceans and the growth of plants, the spreading of plague and the rotation of the earth. Every phenomenon followed a pattern that French described and had causes and consequences that it explained.

But in the mist outside, words had no such power. Short and hushed, soft and muffled, they had no more grasp on anything around me than I. Vowels rolled off the tongue and skimmed lips; mere wisps of air, if that. Longer words collapsed into one stressed syllable while the rest was mumbled and vanished. Their wayward spelling ('thorough', 'through'; 'ghost', 'goose'; 'loose', 'lose') gave little, if anything, of how words sounded. And how they sounded gave no clue on how to spell them, with letters there for no apparent reason ('debt', 'salmon', 'receipt'). With its genderless nouns—its 'you', used to address both your elderly neighbour and your pet—its rules no more fixed than clouds in the wind, English was vague, unpredictable and inconsistent. It could not be trusted to describe with precision what I saw, felt, or thought. It served no purpose and gave no answers to the queries of a shy growing girl who needed certainties. English was but muted background music in that foggy London of my childhood and early teens.

Towards the end of winter, the fog lifted and sheets of rain drenched the city. In late May or early June there came a day—and soon another—when pink clouds strolled across the milky sky and burst into sudden showers. In the morning, the pristine city shone and patches of corn flower blue appeared above the roofs. Parks filled with girls in frocks and boys in shorts; bushes rustled, flowers blossomed. I knew they would soon take me to the Midi, my mum and dad, for the summer months.

After long evenings of hiding and seeking and running in the square, bags were packed, the 2CV loaded and, at the crack of dawn, off we were. We drove along narrow roads, up and down gentle slopes, past rows and rows of red brick terraced houses with no terraces, front gardens overgrown with roses tumbling over wooden fences, sleepy sheep in enclosed soft green fields, thick woods and, sometimes, in the distance, a black church spire pierced a careless cloud.

'There yet, Dad?' I asked, even before we heard the seagulls. 'There yet?'

'Use your eyes,' he'd say, 'and think.'

We heard them screech and saw them wheel at last and, in thick petrol exhaust fumes, the car crawled inside the depths of the ferry's belly. I scrambled up the steep, narrow staircases to reach the top deck, grabbed the banister, stood in the wind and looked. Of course we weren't there yet. It took so long before all the cars were loaded, the gangways pulled in, the thick ropes uncoiled, the siren sounded, the ship heaved, turned and left the harbour. In slate grey choppy waters, she gathered speed at last and headed south towards my country, a country I hardly knew.

I held the roadmap tight as we drove through grey villages and stopped for bland meals in grim cafés. My father sang old French revolutionary songs to keep awake when the sun came down on the northern flatlands and endless open wheat fields that touched the outskirts of the capital city. At the top and centre of the map, like a queen, Paris looked down upon her realm, the rest of the country. She was the place where all roads began and ended. But we always bypassed the city: we were heading south and it was a long way away.

I kept my eye and finger along the red line on the map, peeked for names along the road and when they were identical, in glee, I cried them out and brought my finger down a jot. There we were, going down, getting closer to the Midi. I preferred travelling on the map rather than across a landscape checked by trees lined up like soldiers, or filled with urban clutter, mostly empty, flat and dreary. Below the middle of the map, just before the Col du Grand Bois, my father stopped the car. We were too heavy to climb the steep mountain pass, so my mum sat at the wheel and my dad and I pushed right up to the top. Back in the car, rolling down the mountain at last, I grabbed the map and demanded explanations.

'We're going down, aren't we? But we were going up just now. Why were we going up, hey, Dad? Why? The south's down there on the map, not up.'

My father's brow crumpled and his eyes darkened in the rear-view mirror.

'Read the map and use your brain.'

'But, Dad, I *am* reading the map and I can see the south's down there. And when we go to the Midi, you always say we're going *down* south. But we were going *up* just now. Has it got it all wrong? Is it rubbish then, this map? Hey, Dad, where are we going?'

It drove me mad. The world outside was in contradiction with the map. I felt betrayed and lost.

'Don't be such a fool. In a minute, you'll see, *ça va descendre*.' That meant his hand would come down and slap my face. I never gave him the chance. I shut up on the spot. I was a fool, was I? Well, he'd never hear a word from the fool again. Never, ever. And anyway, my clothes were clinging to my skin, my throat was dry, the engine was deafening and flies and bees were buzzing all around. Shutting out this awful, unfair world, I threw the map at my feet, myself onto the shapeless bags next to me, closed my eyes and dozed off. When I woke, bathed in sweat, I felt a week had passed. Seeing me emerge in the mirror, my father began singing in Provençal.

'De buon matin, ai rescountra lou trin/ De tres grand rei qu'anavoun en voiagi / De buon matin, ai rescountra lou trin/ De tres grand rei dessus lou grand camin.'

I peeped out and blinked. The sky was deep blue, the land red, fields golden, trees a silvery green, the houses white, their roofs orange. Dazzled, I threw myself onto the bags again and shut my eyes tight. But then it was the smells. Like gusts of mistral they blew in: milky, acid, sharp, sweet; the smells of figs and tomatoes and melting tar; of wine and pines and melon; of eucalyptus and mimosa; and, just before the village, the briny sea. When I dragged myself from the car, the raw, coarse reality of things struck in a welter of blinding, deafening, choking assaults on every parched and sweaty part of me. The scorching, searing sun, the shade, darker than the night after the glare of the day, the constant, steady screeching of cicadas, the hopping, crawling, biting thousand insects, the burning stones, the blistering grains of sand, the sticky salt, the pungent smell of iodine: all seized me and wouldn't let go throughout the summer months.

Knocked out in that overflow of life, I ran to my granny's room when the sun was at its zenith. She spent days behind closed shutters, lying on her bed staring at the ceiling. When I hauled myself onto her bed and our eyes met, her lips sketched a smile and, like a lotus flower, her hand opened on the white sheet. I lay by her side and put my hand in hers. She hardly spoke; when she did, she told the weirdest tales in the strangest tongue, a mixture of Provençal and French and, sometimes, I thought I could make out a few of the English words I'd tried to teach her. In answer to 'How are you?' she'd utter a 'Veiouell, zinkyou' that had us in stitches. As years went by, her tales grew fewer and stranger but, even as I reached my teens, I'd find excuses not to join my cousins for stifling, blinding afternoons on the beach and stole to my granny's bed. It was an island, the quietest, sweetest place I knew during those summer months, when everything outside was ablaze, unforgiving and hostile.

If I was French in England, I certainly wasn't French in France. I was *la petite Anglaise* in the village. My cousins and the neighbours' children laughed at my accent, or lack of it, and at my ignorance of local idioms and slang. And I knew nothing of the games they played, the songs they sang, the stories of the times.

'We didn't go to school the day after the bomb alert.'

'His dad was killed in a bomb attack in Oran.'

'A car exploded and all the windows were shattered to pieces in the building next to ours.'

My cousins' stories of bomb alerts and attacks, evacuations and murders made us shake with fear and giggle, hidden under the sheets till dawn. The only bombs I knew were bonfires which, to me, remained 'bomb fires' until, years later, I came across the written word. They set our faces and the cold, foggy November night ablaze with excitement. They followed my first brush with independence, pushing an old pram with a rag doll named Guy around the square and knocking on people's doors begging for a penny to buy firecrackers. Nothing I could talk about to my cousins, when I sensed the violence and fear running through their stories were no joke. But be it the OAS bomb attacks in Algeria and France, or the Catholic's failed attempt at blowing up Parliament in London, I was never completely privy to what was going on. I was a bad fit here and there, in London where I was born and growing up, as well as in Provence where my family came from.

So when I could stop alternating from misty skies to scorching sun, I did. At seventeen, I moved to the grey mineral capital city where for years, I delved into the complexities of my mother tongue. I undid, dismantled, laid bare its spare parts and reassembled them thinking that by doing so, I would reassemble myself and become truly French. And during all those years, I hardly heard or spoke, read or wrote a word of English.

Little did I know. Like a stream waters a meadow beyond its shores, English had seeped through me. I'd heard it in my cradle, as gentle and hushed as a lullaby. I'd tasted it in the small steamy tea room where my mother often took me after school and where I stuffed my face with sponge cake, blancmange, muffins, doughnuts, crumpets, scones, treacle tart, clotted cream, warm custard. I'd inhaled it with the smoke in cinemas and on the upper decks of buses. It had wrapped itself around me like soft wool muffling the voices of the shadows gliding past beneath huge dark umbrellas. It had mingled with the laughter, smoke and music escaping the dark heavy velvet curtains of pubs I walked by. Like things half-seen, half-heard, half-hidden, it was mysterious. And like all things mysterious, it stirred the imagination and begged to be dis-covered. In short, it was desirable.

English was the language of the playground, the backyard, the square, places with no figures of authority, no rules except our own and those of the games we played to the rhythm of the rhymes we sang—'Ring a ring o'roses', 'Eeny, meeny, miney, mo', 'Hickory, dickory, dock'. Nonsense words that made teapots go jibber jabber joo and me take weirdness for granted.

When it was too cold and foggy to play outdoors and school books were back inside the satchel, I'd draw the curtains of my bedroom against the darkness, take my other books off the shelves and prop them all around me against the legs of the bed, desk and wardrobe. I'd sit on the floor and, primed for adventure, be off with Teddy, my teddy bear, and Peter Rabbit and Humpty Dumpty, Georgie Porgie, Little Miss Muffet, Winnie-the-Pooh, Cinderella and Little Red Riding Hood in tow, making up the words I couldn't read beneath the drawings or the pop-ups. And down and down I'd fall, down the rabbit-hole to Wonderland to join the Hatter, the Owl and the Pussycat who went to sea in a beautiful pea green boat, or the cow who jumped over the moon.

'Good morning girls.'

'Good morning, Miss Robinson.'

'Will you say grace, Isabelle, please?'

'For what we are about to receive, may the Lord make us truly thankful. Amen.'

In the mornings, we received porridge and eggs and bacon; in the evenings, pies and puddings, sponges and jellies in the dining room of the school where I was a boarder for a term in my early-teens. I, who had had no religious education and didn't believe in God, said grace and sang hymns during assembly as if I was shaking off an old heavy dress I'd always worn and slipping into a new, fancy one made of a material so light and soft against my skin, it made me feel I was another person. The thrill of it. You flicked your hair to the other side of your head, put on a Panama and striped orange tie and, by the trick of another tongue, there you were in your new attire, slightly chilly at first but getting warmer as you moved around like you'd never done before and sang hymns at the top of your voice, not sure what it all meant but sure it made you feel on top of the world.

I'd stepped out of one frame into another. And there and then, I started paying heed to them, those words I heard, read, sang. Lest they should sneak away, I wrote them down. 'Meekly, dewy, wilderness, hitherto, honeysuckle'. I let them roll around my mouth. 'Willowy, ludicrous, wisteria, bashful, relinquish'. And my throat opened and my tongue explored new areas of my palate. 'Lackadaisical, flabbergasted, supercilious, cantankerous, gobbledegook'. I dared toss a couple in a spoken or written sentence and watched to see where the ripples reached. 'I'm afraid,' I'd drop when there was nothing to be afraid of. 'Glitter, glimmer, glisten, gleam, glint, glow,' I muttered looking for correspondences between light and the sound 'gl'.

My attention was shifting from things to words, from reality to language, its music, pauses, tones and intonations, from sense to sound and back again. I could afford to play and fool around, explore and dig: nothing was at stake, no curriculum, no exams to take, no expectations or judgments, no doubts or fear. But soon, the game was over. I stepped back inside the French frame, pulled on my old heavy dress again, and moved to Paris, not knowing yet that it was possible to have two homes and live in both, to be this, as well as that.

'*Il était une fois…*' had led to ripping stories apart, observing their spare parts, analysing their workings, witnessing the power of mind over matter. 'Once upon a time…' had opened up worlds as dense as ancient forests along whose edges I walked, watching, in awe of the complexity of matter, shadows, mist and wavering shafts of sunlight getting caught in branches and wondering what strange beasts were rustling in the thick undergrowth. While the weeded fields and straight roads of French had offered distant views, the muddy paths and foggy lanes of English I groped my way along had allowed inner landscapes to emerge. It was the other place, the soft-hued mysterious garden I could run to and roam, when light and the arrogance of reason became too strong.

Many years later, when came the time for stories, when I knew you could come from one place *and* another, I half closed the shutters against the sun and the stories, naturally, took shape in the language that was my other home, the one where I'd been free to drift into the realm of dream and fantasy.

The Van

The word QUEEN is stuck in diamond studs on her jeans. She's got her mum's butt and the same swing to her hips. The diamonds are shimmering in the dusk, swaying a few metres ahead. She must be in her thirties. She wasn't even a speck of an idea when I got inside her mum's pizza van, the first, and last, to pull into the village.

The day Gina drove her sky-blue van into our lives I was drawing wine and filling bottles and demijohns at the Co-op. The harvesting had been good and the barrels were full. A shadow blocked the light coming in from the doorway. It gave me such a jolt I dropped the hose and spilt litres of juice on the concrete floor before I managed to stick it back inside the neck and turn the tap off.

    A wine co-operative is a man's world. Women wait in the car while their husbands get their demijohns filled. They give a couple of hoots after a bit and angry little taps on their wrists when the husbands stick their noses outside. But that girl, she just stepped inside, and with the low autumn rays flowing along her curves, she looked me in the eye and fired, 'Hello! Could I have a word with the person in charge?'

    'The person in charge?'
    'Yes. I'd like to speak with him.'

I was in charge. President of the Co-operative. Saw no harm in letting the girl use our fountain, make and sell her pizzas on our car park and settle there for a while. I brought it up at the next general meeting. Old Léon suggested we demand a small rent for letting her moor under the plane tree in our yard. No, I said. Think of the benefits we'll gain from having pizzas on our doorstep. A bonus to our wine. Customers will get two treats in one go.

She had the knack for pizzas, Gina. Rain or shine, they all stopped for one, the builders and the lorry drivers and the sales reps. And when she turned to paint the dough red with crushed tomatoes, they'd lean over the counter and couldn't keep their eyes off those buttocks of hers. 'Arrivederrrrci!' she'd sing as she placed a warm carton on their outstretched arms.

A month after she arrived, I locked the door of the Co-op and walked to the van to say goodnight and get a quick eyeful. She was poking the fire inside the oven.

'Hey! I've got a problem here. The oven's getting cold.'

'I'll fix it,' I said. 'I'll get the fire blazing, don't you worry.' She flicked back a lock of black hair from her brow and her laughter filled the van when I looked up from the burning oven. She pulled down the awning over the counter, closed the back doors of the van and, well, if they were firm to the eye, god, how soft to the touch they were. Those buttocks, as sweet as honey.

During the slow minutes when day slides into night, I'd sit smoking in the kitchen as pictures of Pierrot or Henri having fun inside the van cropped up, and I had half a mind to rush to the Co-op and check to see what she was up to under the plane tree. But Hélène was putting Annie to bed upstairs and the sound of teeny objects dropped, bird-like cries, bits of songs and laughter kept me rooted to my chair. And anyway, I couldn't lock her up in her van, could I?

She was the one to moan sometimes. She turned on the waterworks, chewed at my ear lobe, cried, 'Oh come on, stay a little longer, till the day breaks.' Other days, she'd stamp her feet till the van shook, yell I was selfish, wanted it all and if I didn't at least drive her somewhere on a Sunday, anywhere, she'd just go, go, go, no need to even say ciao, it was easy enough for her to cast off, she had it all in here, her whole life, all she had to do was start the van, she'd done it all her life, start the van and go, oh yes, off she'd be, and I'd never see her again, never ever.

I never saw the dawn break from the tiny lace-curtained windows of her van. Fair's fair. I let her earn her living for free on our car park and she knew it. Plus there was Hélène and Annie, and she knew that too. But nothing's easier than to start a van and go, and stop along the road on someone's doorstep with curves and fiery eyes. So as soon as Hélène started taking Annie on those arty outings the village council organised to visit some museum, old church or Roman ruin, I whisked her off. I roped the boat up on top of the car and when I got to the van, there was Gina, in her sky-blue mini-dress and matching sandals, waving her towel in the rising sun. She propped her transistor radio on top of the glove box and with the wind blowing in our hair, we blinked as pine trees lit up along the road. 'Papa was a rolling stone, wherever he laid his hat was his home,' she sang along with The Temptations, tapping her fingers on my leg. And when the golden bay unfolded before our eyes, she shrieked and squeezed my thigh.

We undid the rope, held the boat up over our heads and, burying our feet just below the burning surface of the sand, glided across the beach till we felt the cool foam tickle our toes. We paddled off, anchored a kilometre out, and the world was ours. She dived between my legs, played the octopus around my chest, lay on my back, her raft she said, and we drifted over the silver waves.

'Right down to Corsica!' I cried.

'No,' she pleaded. 'All the way to Sicily!' We wolfed her golden bread, heaped with anchovies, tomatoes, cheese, olives, sausage; we licked the juice trickling out of peaches and melons off one another's chins. And as we lay naked on the bottom of the boat, softly rocking, a thousand questions tumbled inside my mind about the dazzling island and its dark silhouettes hugging white walls. But her head was rolling in the hollow of my shoulder and she was dozing off. Who would have the heart to wake an almond-tasting sleeping beauty and unfold a past she'd left? I tried, I did. I often tried. But as the sun sank into the sea and set the sky on fire, all I did, just to hear her laughter ripple in the breeze over the waves, was whisper in her ear, 'A sunset's worth a thousand dawns.'

In the dusk, the puzzling sparkles of Sicily gone extinct, I ruffled her hair, sticky with sand and salt, stroked her burning shoulders and looked in amazement at the long shadows of the pine trees along the road. When we got to the van, I couldn't believe we'd left our plane tree only that morning. They were good times. Perhaps the best I ever had.

They built a motorway a couple of kilometres south of the village and the grocers', the bakers', the cobbler's, the cafés closed, one after the other. And a few years later, it was a bypass in the north. The council said our gardens along that new road would be worth a fortune if they could be built on. So we thought what the hell, they're only tiny plots of land with a few old medlar and jujube trees, and half the marrows and the tomatoes we grow we leave to rot anyway, we've got so many. So we sold, and they built their shops. Only Marius, still behind the counter in his bar at seventy-four, stayed on. Cars and caravans and lorries zoomed the motorway and whizzed past the village. And those who took the bypass bought sun cream, sodas and hot dogs and rushed back to the motorway.

Our car park was emptied, save for my car and the pizza van side by side under the plane tree. Squads of backfiring mopeds raced onto the village, drew large noughts and eights in clouds of smoke on the market square and spluttered back to the bypass, leaving dust and silence hanging in the air. Sitting behind her counter, Gina stared at the empty road ahead and didn't start her oven before the church bells chimed midday. When I stepped out, she slowly waved her duster from under the awning, and I rushed back inside and banged my fists on the barrels. All I knew for sure was one of these days, she'd start her van and leave.

She went to the new shops along the bypass and asked around. 'We need parking space for our customers. You can't stay here,' they told her. And one day, the van was gone. We kept looking back towards the plane tree and shook our heads. But I got a postcard at the Co-op one morning. She'd headed west and docked her van a hundred kilometres away, on the outskirts of Aix. I tore along the motorway, went round and round the city's bypass, couldn't find the way out of car parks bigger than our market square, got stuck behind warehouses larger than our church. When I spotted the sky-blue van, it looked a flimsy toy thing at the foot of tower blocks, like huge rockets for midgets. I leaned against a tree and watched, between the men standing at the counter, as she slid a pizza inside a carton, placed it on a pair of outstretched arms, then turned to face the oven, offering them her backside. I cut across the dark to the van and flung the back door open. She gasped. '*Prego*! No more orders. I'm closing early. Got a hell of a lot to do!'

A stream of lorries rumbled past along that road and the van shook. We drove up a narrow lane. Brambles brushed against the car. A skinny cat shot past in the headlights. She gripped my leg. The lane led to a quarry. I got a blanket out of the boot and laid it on the rocks. Dogs howled in the distance. We held on to one another, tighter than ever on that blanket, a raft lost in uncharted seas. 'I can't go on like this,' she said. And a flow of Italian words gushed down my neck until I pressed her wet face into my chest and kept it buried there. 'Gina, Gina, please, Gina, it'll be all right,' was all I could say, over and over.

The first frost seized the earth and the pruning started, then the ploughing and the spraying. After a whole day on the land in gusts of mistral that cut through the body, I simply couldn't make it. But when the wind died, I sped down the motorway. As the kilometres flashed, questions I'd never asked roamed my mind. But it was dark when I got to the van and so warm by the oven I stripped her with my horny hands and we hurried to the floor and hardly talked. One stormy night, as sheets of rain lashed the metal box and crashed onto the roof, she forced me under her, kept me there all along and collapsed on top when she was done. We unlocked our bodies, untangled our fingers and stared at the ceiling in the din. Time was ticking by. I got up, dressed, looked back. She'd pulled a blanket over her body. Her lips were tight, her eyes shut. She didn't turn to me when I opened the door, and I left her there as more clouds burst.

A postcard would come, eager, impatient, demanding. Surely a postcard would come. I raced to the Co-op in the morning, slammed the door of the empty letterbox, filled a demijohn in the cellar, opened a file in the office, ran to the front door when I heard an engine stop outside, usually Pierrot or Henri. And when they left, I did it all again, filling a bottle, emptying another, opening a file, banging a door shut, charging around like a blind bull in a ring. No postcard came. 'Got business to do in town,' I told Pierrot one morning. I belted down the fast lane of the motorway but when I got to the tower blocks, there were only empty cans lying under the dusty trees and a few soiled and scattered pizza cartons.

I took the old winding road back to the village, drove along each bypass, U-turned and went around each market square. I stopped at every wine co-operative. 'Seen a sky-blue pizza van by any chance? The girl, Gina's her name, she forgot a bag on our car park. Got it here in the boot.' I'll track her down, I groaned. I'll find her, squeeze her in my arms and ask her when and why she left her island and how she came to live in that van and who taught her how to knead that dough and if there were lemon and almond trees in her garden and what roads she'd taken before she docked under our plane tree. Things will come together and I will build a dry dock for her floating life. When the Co-op appeared in the headlights, I swear I saw a shadow stealing past the plane tree onto the road, and a strange pain crept inside my chest and weighed a ton.

I'd read about it in the paper, her marriage to the grocer, the twerp who'd settled for the bypass and had become manager of the supermarket. I saw her walking across the church square once, pushing a pram. I buried the sight inside a corner of my mind until that afternoon at the post office. She was ahead of me in the other queue. My eyes got caught inside the nest of black curls that coiled on her slender neck and glided down her back to the golden ribbon of skin between her top and jeans, and lower still, to the curves in the small of her back, so tender where the buttocks swell. I felt them inside the palms of my hands, those curves, and the tastes of almond and honey welled inside my mouth and filled my throat till I choked. I edged out of the line, out of the post office and all the way to the Co-op. The bitch, oh, the bitch, I hissed, she won't get away with it, oh, the bloody bitch.

I had other things on my mind, thank god. The Co-operative was agonising. We'd thought the motorway would open up the world—an outlet for our wine. But it opened up our land to the world and killed us in the process. They got the job done fast, those northern sods who thought black olives grew on black olive trees and rosé wine was red and white mixed. They scurried down that motorway, flooded our plains and started settling on our land. They built white boxes with bright red roofs for them to warm their arses and huge grey plastic boxes for them to buy their junk, their plastic chairs, canned beans, beers. They turned our canals off their courses to fill big blue pools to cool their bums. And they liked it here so much they wanted to extend their settlements, those northern bastards from north European monarchies. They decreed no new vine could be planted and those we had should be pulled out. They paid a handful of figs so our rich red land, the best in the world, should lay fallow. Even when the mistral howls down the mountains, unleashes its gusts onto the plain, crashes against the rows of cypress, fools over the roofs and blows the horns off bulls, even then, after days of this hullabaloo, it leaves our land undisturbed, it's so rich and heavy.

The day the last vine was pulled from my six acres, the air was quiet. I stood under the fig tree. It screeched and shuddered. A flock of crows took off from its limbs, swooped onto the blood-red furrows for their feast of worms and mice, and plucked at the soil, naked now, skinned, its veins exposed. I had to wipe my eyes on my sleeve to back the car onto the road and leave.

'Sell it,' Hélène said. 'Start selling.' I grunted. 'Sell it. Sell some of it at least,' she said again. I groaned. I picked the figs and brought them home but then left them for the crows to pluck and I kicked at the weeds, the nettles, the brambles taking over the whole bloody place.

'What's the point in going on your twice-yearly inspection of growing disaster?' Hélène sneered. 'Sell it, you fool.'

At the Co-operative we made piles of crates and sacks, of old labels, old bills and old ledgers until we had nothing left, but to face it. No vines, no wine, no Co-operative. We held our last general meeting amongst the scraps, Pierrot, Henri and me. The Co-op closed, its windows boarded, the tractors sold, and the barrels, presses, scales, left to rust and rot.

They said my vineyard could be divided into a dozen plots, the buggers who poured their smiles on me in their air-conditioned office along the bypass. And they could build a dozen 'villas' they said, looking big. They got these two ninnies in from the city. One peered inside a lens on a tripod and held his hand up to the other who held his up in answer. Weeks later, the real estate buggers laid a large sheet of paper on their desk, 'This is how it should be divided.' They pointed thin, bony fingers at what they called the best 'product', the plot along the road that goes up to the mountains, just before the crossroads. It was sold in no time. I didn't go to the notary to sign the deeds. Gave my proxy to one of the real estate buggers. Avoided going there after. Would make me sentimental. A bloody waste of time.

We went up for the wild boar on a crisp winter morning with Henri and his dog in his 2CV. Crazy's tongue was dripping over my shoulder. I turned to give him a slap on the muzzle just before the crossroads and glanced out of the window. There, the fig tree gone, a black expanse of tar instead, two cars and a sky-blue van parked alongside a big white box with a bright red roof. Henri was a cautious driver. He pressed the brake long before he knew there was a stop, and I had all the time in the world to soak it in. A young girl ran out carrying a school bag. She settled in a car. A man followed and then a woman in a blue coat. She flicked back a lock of black hair from her brow, sat at the wheel. The twerp closed her door, waved. She hooted briefly twice, shot off, didn't see us come, slammed on the brakes. We stopped. She zoomed past and turned towards the village. And she was gone.

Henri pulled over and kept his hand on the horn for a good three minutes. When he got back to gripping the wheel, he shouted, 'See that bird?' I stared ahead at the grey mountains. 'Doesn't know what she's doing. See that? Won her licence in a raffle.' I stared ahead. 'Looked a lot like our pizza girl,' he muttered.

'You going to stay here all day?' I barked. He changed into first gear and we started uphill until he reached his racing speed of forty kilometres an hour.

'Blimey. On your land. Did you know?'

'Get a move on, will you. At this rate, we won't get there before the end of the blinking hunting season.'

'All right, all right. But did you see that bird?'

The light was slanting across the red plain and the crows were cawing and flapping across the sky as we came down from the mountains. Though we'd rolled the roof open, the car was full of the smells of wine and sweat and blood. Crazy was snoring on top of two wild pigs and a roe deer at the back. As always when he had a few under his belt, Henri was down to thirty kilometres an hour. He'd started humming a short while back. As we approached the crossroads, he flapped up his window and boomed, *'Ami entends-tu le vol noir des corbeaux dans la plaine?'** He slapped the steering wheel and stepped on the gas. The engine roared and we took off. I banged my window up and a smell of moist earth blew into our faces. I got my rifle from the back of the car and held it pointing to the sky. *'Ce soir l'ennemi connaîtra le prix du sang et des larmes,'** we sang at the top of our voices. Henri gave a hoot in tune on each syllable and I started shooting at the crows. A couple dropped. Crazy was barking like a mad dog. Just before we got to the white box with the red roof, I stood, placed a knee on my seat and, above Henri's head, aimed and fired. I reckon I stuck a good few bullets into the back of that sky-blue van.

I often broke into a sweat in the middle of the night after that day, and the thought of it kept me awake till dawn. She could have been inside the van. She might have kept it for her pizzas. She could have been pulling one out from the oven when the bullets hit the back doors and their tiny windows. I told myself I'd have heard about it. Couldn't be sure though. She wasn't from the village. But Hélène looked up from her paper one morning.

'Over and done with,' she said.

'What?'

'A life. Done and over with.'

'Who?'

'That vulgar pizza girl you kept on the car park at the Co-operative. Says here she was tearing down the motorway in her van. No one else involved.'

Just like usual we crowded into the church square when the bell tolled, stomachs knotting, fearing who kicked the bucket. A stranger with luck, or one of the old black marketeers no one's got time for, and off we'll go. But if the name, swiftly passed around the square, rings a bell, we stick together and standing there, waiting for the women to come out of the church, we pull stories from the air to patch up the holes in our threadbare memories.

'Born in 1926, was he?'

'No, '27.'

'You say he worked down at the greenhouse? No, still can't place him.'

'He nearly scorched that summer our woods were reduced to ashes.'

'Good lord, of course! His aunt Marie sold my father land down by the river. Just before the war it was.'

'His heart, was it? Was always a bit of a weedy

specimen, he was.'

And they're back again, our old school mates, alive and kicking for the time it takes to walk the lane to the cemetery. But where she'd flown in from, our pizza girl, no one ever knew for sure, and our gathering dwindled away. The twerp, the daughter and a couple of girls her age stood outside the church and, opposite Marius's bar, were the meagre male leftovers, Pierrot, Henri and me.

"Twas handy having her van on our car park, wasn't it?' Henri croaked, shooting me a dark glance. Caught Pierrot giving a few slight nods. But if they too had stepped inside that van, it was too late to start on this. We were balding now, stooping, panting, the three of us, and I looked away towards the mountains. We tugged at our stiff shirt collars and keeping our distance from the twerp and the daughter, we started behind the black van towards the cypress trees.

QUEEN's glittering in the twilight. The girl hasn't a clue who I am, what I meant to her mum. She must have seen me around though. Perhaps her mum gave her a nudge at the market. 'See that guy over there, well, you know, years and years ago, before you were born, we...' Nah. You don't say such things to a daughter. Perhaps she caught a glimpse that day, fifteen, no, god, sixteen years ago, standing waiting by the black van in the square. She's nearly reached the church now. Thought she was her mum for a second, hurried a little, the pain in my knee gone, nearly went up to her, nearly grabbed her arm.

I could speak to her. Perhaps I should. I knew your mum, I'd start. She'd turn to me wide-eyed. And I would tell her if she finds it strange the way they slip a little further away from you each day, those who've gone for good, well I could help. If she finds it's getting lonelier with her memories wilting, I could offer a few of mine. I'd tell her all about the softness of her mum's curls, like down on the nape of her neck. And how her laughter rippled over the silver-blue wavelets. And how the cork popped out of the bottle of champagne and made a dent on the ceiling of the van, the champagnes I'd brought to celebrate her first and second years under our plane tree, the champagne she poured all over me. And how she lapped it up. She may not recognise her mum in those recollections, but they'd put some new life back into her. And like a distant star, she'd shine out there, her mum would.

Oh, shut up you old fool. Don't be daft. And anyway, I couldn't catch up with QUEEN, swaying though she is, even if I wanted. She's reaching the church and the pain shoots through my knee. Damn. Hélène's right about taking a walking stick.

There's a dim light inside Marius's bar. Could stop for a drink and rest my knee. I peer inside to see who's there. An old, hunched man limping along is reflected in the window. God, that's me. I stumble on the pavement, fall on my bad knee.

'You all right?' She's walking back towards me. I grunt, try to get back on my feet, but the bloody knee gives. 'There, let me help.' She bends over and grabs my arm. I shake her off. I crawl to the wall and scramble up holding on to a shutter. 'I'll walk you home.'

'No, no, I'm all right. I'm fine, fine.'

'Suit yourself,' she says and walks away. I lean against the wall, panting, gripping the shutter. Her hips are swaying down the narrow alley under the arches along the church. The old pain in my chest is back and weighs a ton. QUEEN shimmers in the dark. And she is gone.

---

* From 'le Chant des Partisans'

That Girl

'That girl, do you know her?' Jim asks Victor.

The girl's slowly swaying her hips in tight jeans across the square towards the stairs that lead to the main street.

'I've seen her around. Don't know her though. Why?'

'Just wondered. She comes in and helps my wife around the house. Cleaning, ironing, things like that.'

A cloud blocks the sun adding hours to the day in a second. The afternoon Paris-Nice swishes along behind the poplar trees. The girl walks up the stairs and disappears in the street.

'Quite a stunner, isn't she?'

Victor takes his time to fill his pipe and light it.

'Guess so,' he answers, lost in the smoke eddies.

'My wife likes her. Says she's had a hard life.'

More clouds roll in and to the south, the Rochebrune Mountain is turning dark purple. The swishing of the train dies out and the muffled roar from the motorway beyond the railway track takes over and invades the plain. That's the only time you hear that roar, for a minute or two, after the train's gone by, and then you forget about it because it's always there.

'Her mother died in a car crash when she was eighteen,' Jim says. But Victor's sure the girl wasn't eighteen when Gina died on the motorway. Fifteen, sixteen perhaps, but not eighteen.

They're sitting on a bench in front of the old washhouse. Victor, the tall one, has been coming to the square since he was a boy, standing on his granny's pushcart for her weekly rides to the washhouse, holding on to her basketful of linen. When the wind blew off a handkerchief from the top of the pile, he caught it in mid-air, put it back on top and flung himself across the basket to keep it there. A real joy ride with the bumps, stones and potholes on the way. It was seventy years or so ago.

Jim is younger. He used to teach French in North London. When the school stopped offering the subject, he felt so hurt he refused to beg for a post elsewhere. His love of French—a love that never failed him, born in a classroom when he was eleven—rejected, crushed and trampled. He took early retirement, sold his possessions and crossed the Channel with his wife, heading south to buy a house and plot of land just outside the village two years ago.

In spring, Victor and Jim watch the *pétanque* players in the square and are on nodding terms. When summer comes, they exchange words on the heat and the game. As the plane trees shed leaves, the players move to the café for card games. But even when there's a nip in the air, even when there's a drizzle, Victor tells Hélène, 'I'm going for a walk. Need anything?' When he gets to the top of the stairs above the square, he squints towards the washhouse. If the benches are empty, he buys grated cheese or tobacco and saunters home. If Jim is there—he often is—Victor forgets his bad knee and finds himself down the stairs in next to no time.

When the Paris-Nice whizzes past and dusk creeps, he can't believe how fast time went. He finds it odd. Jim's a stranger, a stranger from the North. He wears a raincoat, brings a paper to the bench, an umbrella sometimes. His vowels roll off his tongue. He laughs his head off at some of the words Victor uses. Amused and eager, his eyes dart right and left. But he's keen to know about the village. And now, the stranger knows Gina's daughter, who swings her hips just like her mother did, and he thinks she's a stunner.

At night, Jim listens to the sough of the wind in the pine trees behind the house on his small plot on a swelling of the land. When the smell of resin and mist rise at dawn, he feels on shifting sands, not yet anchored. To shake the feeling, he grabs his spade and digs. He unearths cut stones and broken tiles, rusty bolts, nails, keys, thick ivy roots as tough as iron, scattered remains of a past of which he knows nothing. He kicks at fragments, says this plot is just wasteland, can't do a thing with it. He hoes up the weeds along the two rows of vines on the top terrace and does a bit of pruning, but not a leaf unfurls when spring breaks out. They're like scorched arthritic hands, those vines, begging the sky for help. He'll have to pull them out. He plants a row of cypress trees near the gate, they do not last the year; honeysuckle and lupins along the house, but nothing grows. Nothing's taking root.

If he knew more about this soil, about the way the elders worked, fed and watered it, if he could summon up a picture of past days, then perhaps he could begin to make them his, this house and plot, and feel he's docked at last. He brings his paper to the square in the afternoon, but hopes there'll be a villager sitting on a bench, ready for a chat. Victor perhaps, that tall man with soft grey-blue eyes in a craggy face, who smokes a pipe, sounds the final vowels he'd always thought were silent, and whose hands, like busy birds, flutter and whirl about him while he talks.

'C'était comment?' Jim asks, *"Dites, c'était comment, la vie au village?'*

'I'll tell you. I'll tell you how things were. Your business was words, wasn't it? You can produce words anytime and anywhere. Even at night, in an empty room, even in the middle of a desert, you can jabber away. But, you see, everything we do, everything we have, we do or have because of this.' Victor makes a sweeping gesture that reaches to the sky, his hand opening as if offering a view he owned.

And he tells Jim about the cork oak trees that grew from the brow of the mountains, so the elders made corks and floaters, mats and panels. And gorse sprang from the river banks, so they made baskets and fences and awnings. Because pine tree forests covered the mountains and hills, horses, and later lorries, soon moved up and down loaded with pine logs. So planks and crates, tables and barrels were made. Even before the First World War, women could find jobs nailing crates at the saw mill down by the river. And because sun and streams fed and watered the plain, the soil craved for vines and fruit, and the Romans planted vineyards and orchards, with loads to spare.

Victor gets carried away wanting Jim to see that men and land are one here. Never before has he told these stories, the kind that sweep across the centuries and take you sailing upstream on a river whose source is so remote no one can find it. When he's with his old pals, Henri and Pierrot, the two that are still around, they hardly ever start on that journey. They don't go far when they do, and there's no end of quibbling and squabbling.

'That mildew, in 1956? Don't be daft. I know for sure it was in 1957.'

'Léon wasn't president of the Co-op the year the vines were blighted by frost. Course he wasn't. Alphonse was.'

They take short, safe paths to what the doctor said

the day before, or what the mayor claimed he'd do last spring about the diseased plane trees on the square, eaten up by canker. They bet on who'll fall first, the trees or them. But that outsider from the North, he wants to be taken all the way upstream. He listens, laughs and begs for more as Victor pulls bygone days out of cobwebs. And Victor would go on and on if it wasn't for the strain that wafts in the air when that girl, who never looks their way, rolls her hips across the square. As the roar from the motorway takes over, Victor taps his pipe against the bench to let the ash fall and mutters something about the cold dampness that rises from the river and reawakens the pain in his knee. Jim buttons up his coat and they part with a brief, '*A bientôt*', knowing the tales aren't over.

Winter sets in. Under the bare plane trees, facing the low mean sun over the Rochebrune Mountain, Jim begins to form a picture of past days. But he's eager for the strokes to be defined, dabs of colour added, people, movement.

'*Et la mer, si proche?*'

'The sea? At the end of the summer, before the rush at dawn to the vineyard for the picking, we watched the sky from time to time to check it wasn't gathering dark clouds. And if we reckoned it wouldn't turn wild and destroy a year's labour, we left the grapes to swell and sweeten a couple of days, a week at most, and went to the sea for the day. We smelt it before we saw it and knew how huge the catch would be. And when its deep cobalt blue and the golden sand filled the windscreen, it swept us off our feet.'

'*Et les vignes?*'

'The vines? At the heart of our lives.'

Victor's speech is tinged with pride when he sails upstream again and explains that to keep up with the times, the elders had to expand the old Roman vineyards on their fat lush land, and they needed tractors, bigger presses and barrels to develop the subtleties of their juices. So between the two Wars, they got together and built a wine co-operative where each man's vote counted just the same, whether his land was the size of a pocket-handkerchief or an American plantation.

'We shared it all at the Co-operative: machines, work force, worries.'

'Where is it?'

'Gone. Closed down in the nineties. Torn down a few years later. Razed to the ground.'

Victor raises both arms and lets them drop on his lap.

Dark clouds wander in from the mountain. They watch the Paris-Nice whizz past to the end of the row of poplar trees. The roar of the motorway fades into oblivion, and the day Gina appeared on the Co-op's doorstep blusters in—Gina, with low golden rays around her curves and black fiery eyes. And as the girl goes by swinging her hips, Victor can't help asking, 'That girl, still comes to your place?'

'Oh, yes. My wife and her, they've become friends of sorts. She tells me a little about her every now and then.' Victor stares in the distance, motionless.

'She doesn't know who her father is.'

A biker revs his engine in the car park below the washhouse. Zooming up the bend into the main street, his leg nearly touching the tarmac, he thunders by. Victor holds his breath waiting for Jim to weave on.

'Damn fool,' Jim says as the muffled roar of the motorway fills the plain.

'The man who'd brought her up, well, after her mother died in that car crash, he told her he wasn't her father, and left. She found herself on her own, aged eighteen. Tough, hey?'

A few large drops of rain crash onto the ground and Jim slaps his knees and rises from the bench. '*A bientôt*', he says, leaving Victor to unfold a body that has never felt so rusty and heavy. He hardly feels the rain. It slides over him as faintly as the years since Gina's death. If he's not the father, that twerp who became manager of the supermarket and married Gina, so what about him then, the father? Who's he? Who? She can't have been eighteen that girl when Gina died, can she? She can't.

Rain falls for days. The minute a ray pierces the clouds, Victor hurries to the square, trying to figure out how and when and what he'll ask Jim to find out more. From the top of the stairs he peers towards the old washhouse. But Jim's not there. On a clear, windy day, he's there at last, sitting reading his newspaper on a bench. As briskly as he can, Victor limps across the square, decides he'll wait till the girl appears before asking, he's not sure what. Jim folds his paper when he sees Victor, and hardly waits until he's settled on the bench.

'You never had to decide or choose a thing, did you?' There's harshness in Jim's tone.

'What do you mean?'

'You didn't choose any of this. This land that yields it all, this land of plenty lined with gold, this sea swarming with fish, this heaven on earth, this wonderland, it was handed down to you. You simply took it.'

Looking away from Jim, Victor lights his pipe. He stares in the distance towards the mountain.

'Of course, we took it. Our fathers' lives were shaped by this land, their hopes and ambitions spring from it. They expected us to improve and develop what they'd built, and pass it down. We had to live up to their dreams. What's wrong with this?'

'Nothing. Except that you didn't have a thing to do to have what you have.'

'What do you know about our lives, you trader in words? You leave your small grey island and land here.

But you could board that train and go to Italy if the fancy took you. You don't understand a thing about our lives. You're unmoored. Rootless.'

Victor clenches his jaw and rises from the bench. He taps his pipe in the palm of his hand to let the ashes fall, briefly nods at Jim and limps across the square with dust whirling around him.

Winter's endless. The mistral unleashes its gusts, slapping and lashing. When it dies, sheets of rain crash onto the plain, then mist covers it right up to Jim's house. The village looks drowned. Only the top of the church tower floats above the mist. Declaring she'd rather die than spend the rest of winter here, Jim's wife goes back to England. If he were on a raft adrift in mid-ocean, Jim wouldn't feel more lost. When there's a lull in the fury of the sky, he rushes to the square. But only small groups of hooded boys hang around the benches. He looks inside the café, recognises some of the summer *pétanque* players standing in clusters at the counter or slapping cards around a table, shrouded in thick smoke. But Victor's nowhere to be seen. Jim spoke harshly for no good reason and Victor must be hurt. Walking back home, he thinks of soft grey skies and gentle breezes, sunny spells and scattered showers, and the smell of wet grass brings a lump to his throat.

Victor didn't like being told they always had it good and easy and all they had to do was step inside their fathers' shoes. He tells Hélène he's off for a stroll in the afternoon, but he turns his back to the Rochebrune Mountain. He takes the old paths that run along olive groves and vineyards and peter out into pinewoods, mulling over what that Jim guy said. What did he mean?

That no better than old dogs, they sniff around trailing the smell of kith and kin, and scrape the same patch over and over to unearth old bones? That like tribesmen, they carry on forever, believing their ancestors' souls are buried in sacred land? That, in short, they're stuck in a rut—a golden rut?

Thinking of old dogs and tribes, Victor finds himself in a pinewood, at the back of a house he doesn't recognise for a minute. It's old Léon's house. A good thing old Léon, who's been dead at least twenty years, isn't here for the sight on the upper terrace. Two rows of dead vines. You pull them out quick, for Christ's sake; burn them and scatter the ashes to feed the soil. A woman appears on the terrace carrying a linen basket. It's her. That girl. He takes a few steps backwards, deeper into the shade, and leans against the trunk of a pine. The girl pulls a white sheet from the basket, throws it over the washing line and begins to stretch it. A man appears. Jim. It's Jim. He pulls the sheet to the other side of the line. The girl places clothes pegs. Jim's shadow moves behind the sheet towards the girl and grabs her hand. Large drops of sunlight fall and play on the sheet flapping and billowing in the wind. The shadows meet and melt onto the ground.

Bastard. If he had his rifle, Victor'd shoot. That guy, he lands here, buys a plot, tries growing lupins— lupins, for god's sake—thinks he'll play *pétanque* next summer and meanwhile, fucks Gina's daughter. Putting down his dangling roots all right, the rat.

Confused and exhausted, Victor limps along the path, muttering. He feels a hundred. He can't erase the sight of the moving bodies behind the white sheet. But a night comes back and superimposes over the scene. The night he held the girl's mother tight, on a blanket, in a quarry. And she clutched and gripped him as if he were her lifebuoy, and talked and talked. He never knew what Gina said that night. He never asked her what those words meant. But there was one he understood all right;

the word 'bambino', repeated again and again till he crushed her wet face into his chest to stop the flow of words and tears.

Victor steps out of the pinewood into the sun-drenched vineyards. By the time he gets to the edge of the village, his mind is set. He'll wait for the girl to appear at the top of the stairs and make her look up at him. And he'll check to see what's there.

He watches her swaying her hips across the street and as she steps onto the pavement, he bumps into her as if he hadn't seen her come. He grabs her arms and looks into the eyes he's always ignored and shunned. They are as blue and round as his used to be. As blue and huge as Annie's.

Annie

The year Annie went to the lycée, they started a photo workshop. She joined it and began to aim and shoot at streams of cars on the motorway, rows of bottles at the supermarket, planes in the sky, her friends at school, their hands, backs, feet, nonsense of the sort.

'That's what I want to do,' she said over and over. In her final year, she often left the table before the meal was over.

'I've told you a hundred times,' she'd hiss, fists clenched on either side of her plate, frowning at her mother, then her father. 'Don't you understand? I can't stay. There's no future for artists in this hole.'

She banged her fists on the table, stomped to her bedroom, slammed the door, and Hélène quietly sobbed. Artists! As if they needed artists in a place like theirs. They fed people, for Christ's sake, quenched their thirst with subtle juices, built their homes and furniture. Vital things that left no time for entertaining sissies. But after her *baccalauréat* and a summer of outbursts, tears and slamming doors, they gave in, and she went up to Paris to take a two-year course in photography. They sent her a monthly allowance for upkeep. She came back to visit, twice the first year, once the next.

Click clack click clack went her high heels on the flagstones on those visits. She never took her shoes off. She looked like an undertaker with her black shoes, her black trousers, her black T-shirt, and walked back and forth from her bedroom to the bathroom like a furious headmistress down a school corridor. Click clack click clack. Each step, the blow of a hammer on Victor's head. But if he asked, 'Please take off your shoes, it gives me a blinking headache,' he knew how she'd stop mid-step, turn with eyebrows arched in bewilderment, plant her huge blue eyes on his, and shoot, 'What? My shoes? They give you a headache? What are you talking about?'

'Do you really need to keep those shoes on while you're in the house?' he ventured once. She didn't stop, or turn, or look at him, but simply threw a curt, 'Yes' over her shoulder, and click clack click clack, was off to her bedroom.

It wasn't that long ago, was it, when the little girl she was ran to him barefoot, pitter patter pitter patter. When he heard, 'Daddy, Daddy, where are you?' and, like raindrops falling on plane tree leaves, her soft round feet on the flagstones, pitter patter pitter patter, all around the house. Had he dreamed it? Had he dreamed the times when she took his hand and led him to the garden to watch a butterfly sipping nectar from a zinnia? He held his breath and slowly stooped and crouched till he was level with Annie and the butterfly, and all were tipsy with sugar, sun and pleasure.

In the last days of August, that chubby, giggling, swirling little girl of his would start pleading, 'Let's go to the sea tomorrow, please, Dad.' And the day the answer was yes, the house shook from the rafters to the cellar. Feet ran up and down the stairs, doors slammed shut and open. Words bounced, echoed in the staircase, flitted in and out of the kitchen, the cupboards, the attic, the garden shed.

'Who's pinched my sandals?'
'Do we want one fishing rod or two?'
'We'll come back with a dolphin.'

'A dolphin? You joking? A whale.'
'Put the masks in the basket.'
'Let's leave at dawn.'
'Go and pick a few tomatoes, I'll boil some eggs.'
'Can I take my new straw hat?'
'Don't forget to put the alarm on.'

At the break of dawn, Victor sang that old song about the three kings and their retinue who rise bright and early and, in their jerkins, set off on the highway to travel and conquer the world. Hélène and Annie joined in, but on the way, after a stifling, sleepless night, they begged to lie for a minute or two in the shade of a pine tree, on a slab of red rock smoothed by rain and wind. But when you were off to the sea, you were off to the sea. What would anyone be doing lying under a bough, when the sea was so near, at the tip of your fingers, beyond that hill. No, silly, look, just after the bend, the bridge and the chapel below. As red as blood in parts, the red of brick dust in others, ochre here and there, the landscape flashed by. And over the slow, muddy river, sometimes, a pink flamingo would spread its wings and take to the sky. Down a silver-green tunnel of laurels and mimosas, catching a glimpse of a lapis lazuli stone shimmering below a dome of hazy blue, Annie shrieked and clapped. They let the boat glide from the roof of the car over their heads and she guided them along the tunnel, running ahead, hopping back, drawing figures of eight between them, slapping her father's paunch and her mother's buttocks as she closed the loops. Victor lashed the lower eucalyptus branches with his fishing rod chanting, 'Here we come, here we come,' to warn the sea urchins, squid and octopuses.

'I'll be gone to Corsica and back before you know it,' he told his women. Annie slapped the wavelets, shook and yapped like a puppy before she grabbed the fishing rod and oars, and launched the boat.

'Look out,' cried Hélène, 'he'll be making waves

right across to Africa with his webbed feet.'

When he crawled back up the rocks he had a basket full of sea urchins and an octopus, tentacles writhing in the sky, planted on the forks of his trident. Hélène and Annie shouted, 'Here comes Neptune, look, the ruler of the waves, here he comes.'

All the children on the stony beach ran to watch him wrestling with the beast, plunging his fingers in the flesh of its slimy body. They stifled cries behind their hands and took a few steps backwards as its tentacles gripped his wrist and its suckers clutched his skin. And then he held the octopus high up above his head and crashed and smashed it on a rock till it lay limp. Holding hands, curling their toes over the stones, ready to scamper back, the children craned their necks to watch in awe as Victor placed the dead monster in a hole in the rock to turn its pocket inside out, and let the ink fill the water with black clouds. The proudest girl on the beach, Annie stood aside, smiling. On the way back to the village, sticky, burning and exhausted, they hummed the old song about the three kings who were off to conquer the world. What an easy conquest the world was then.

When she turned twelve, thirteen perhaps, Annie's round cheeks narrowed. She stopped hopping and running to the sea. She left the boat and fishing rod lying on the beach and hardly dipped a foot in the water. She began to lift her chin up and hold her head the way her mother did, towards the sun. She looked away from Victor's little triumphs on the rock, and gazed and gazed at the horizon.

Perhaps it was there and then, as she sat scanning the horizon, that Annie began to sense that there was more than village. Perhaps she felt as if their little world was covered with a veil which muffled voices, blurred views, dampened colours and limited movements. And the moment she saw the sea and infinite horizon appear at the end of the tunnel of leaves, the veil blew off and, in sharp focus, the world lit up and she began to long for other landscapes.

They went to Paris to visit her a year after she finished her course. On the night they arrived, she took them to what she called a 'cool' restaurant. She kissed the boss. The waiters winked at her. It was stiflingly hot and so dark they couldn't make out what was on their plates. At the table next to theirs, four men wearing sunglasses remained silent for the best part of their meal. The music was loud and steps echoed on the wooden boards. Hélène and Annie tried out sentences in the semi-darkness, cocked their heads to hear the answers and, defeated, raised their hands palms up. When they got up to get their coats, Annie stayed behind for a minute to talk to the men with sunglasses. One of them patted her arm and said something that made them all turn around, look in her parents' direction, and laugh.

She'd booked them a room for the week in a small hotel in a quiet street off the busy one where she rented a flat. They weren't invited to her flat.

'It's so tiny,' she'd laughed, 'it couldn't hold the three of us.' She looked like an urban undertaker, with her black suit and black painted nails. Her lips were shiny red. Victor's granny would have described those lips as a hen's arse with piles. And under her tight black T-shirt, he saw her bra straps were like leopard skin.

When they got back to their hotel room, Victor leaned on the narrow chest of drawers and undid his tie. Hélène sat on the bed, pulled off her stiff patent shoes and rubbed her feet. Under the harsh light falling from the ceiling, he saw the deep lines on her brow and around her eyes and mouth. He hadn't noticed it in the village, the way the years had marked her face.

'Tomorrow, we'll stroll around the area and find a restaurant to our liking,' he said. Hélène went on rubbing her feet and didn't answer. He wondered what she made of the acquaintance their daughter had with the boss and the waiters, and with the men wearing sunglasses in the dark.

The next day they sat in the small hotel lobby under the fronds of a potted palm tree, thumbing tattered magazines, waiting for Annie. She was late and the old fear sneaked in, that something had happened, that she might not come back when she was out at night with weedy guys from the photo workshop at school, not home at midnight. He hated the weakness his thoughts revealed. He'd never voiced his fears and as years went by, his silence had forced his wife's. When he saw the quiver of Hélène's lower lip and the tremor of her hands, he clenched his jaw and examined the back page of an old magazine.

Whirling, flustered, glowing, Annie arrived, an hour late. As if it had been suspended in the waiting, the sight of her blew life back inside him and he could breathe again. Her pretty face was flushed, her eyes shining, her voice high-pitched.

'Let's go to the same place as last night, shall we?'

'No, we're taking you out tonight.'

She looked annoyed for a second but managed a smile.

They'd walked all morning along busy grey streets, studying menus, comparing prices, peering inside restaurants. The one they'd chosen was quiet and brightly lit. After ordering, they began sentences that collided. When their eyes met, they exchanged small smiles that stiffened on their lips, and looked away. Hélène passed a finger around her plate, flicking off specks of dust that weren't there. Annie fiddled with the stem of her wine glass and looked at the photos on the wall, a field in spring, a snow-capped mountain, and a close-up of a black and blue butterfly drinking from a yellow zinnia. Victor glanced at Annie and saw her eyes glide over the butterfly on the zinnia, pass to the window and fix on the traffic outside. And he knew that from then on, he would be alone with the memory of the most precious moments in his life. He took a piece of bread, made little balls with its soft part, pressed them hard on the white table cloth, and turned them into balls again.

They didn't see much of their daughter during their stay. She was busy taking photographs, working freelance, she said. They strolled around and Hélène put her arm inside his. They hadn't walked that way for decades. Her arm felt awkward and heavy but he left it there and she pulled him this way and that to look into shop windows. You couldn't always tell what these shops sold.

'Oh, look. It's Kyoto, isn't it? Perhaps Annie took it,' cried Hélène.

In the window there was a large photo of a cherry tree in full bloom next to a dark red temple and, on the floor in front, perched on a small cardboard box, a pair of pink shoes no one could walk in. He gazed at the cherry tree and the ridiculous shoes, and shook his head.

She chose to turn away from the full bloom of their cherry trees, his girl. She fled the recurring shafts of beauty of their land. She didn't care a fig about the slanting autumn evening light pouring honey over the red vineyards, the wisteria tumbling over gates in spring, the butterflies sipping nectar from lavender, lilac, or zinnias. They didn't keep her. Soil was merely dirt and mud. She never let it grip her feet, weigh and pin her down. She chose to flee.

Victor and Jim are sitting under the shade of the plane trees, on the bench in front of the old washhouse. The Paris-Nice swishes along and the muffled roar from the motorway invades the plain. Victor looks away towards the Rochebrune Mountain and shakes his head.

'My daughter?' He shrugs and takes his time

lighting his pipe before he answers. 'No, no. She doesn't come anymore. We've had no news for a while.'

'A while?'

'Yes. It must be seven years. No. It's eight now. We don't mention Annie anymore. Too painful for Hélène to mention her, or hear her mentioned. She's travelling around the world, I'm sure, taking photos, just the way she wanted.'

The Madman

The madman looks towards the mountains behind me. Not at anything, just the air we never think about unless it whirls and wraps around our bodies. And then it's the forgotten waste in the village we fight. Dried leaves, twigs, bits of glass, of tiles, confetti, empty cans, plastic bags rattling, swirling up, swishing past. But the air is still today. He is holding his usual vigil on the quiet emptiness, leaning against a wall on the step of my neighbour's doorway. I slow my pace a little as I approach, watching. His eyes rest on mine and come alive, round, keen, shimmering.

'I'm so sorry about what happened. Your sister now. After all the rest.' I smile briefly, look away and press on, not wanting to hear more. I have no sister. I hurry to the market square, past the war memorial, and pop over to the chemist's to buy aspirin.

He has turned around now, away from the mountains, body tense, slightly inclined, arms stiff against his legs, a mime's illustration of expectation. I must have been on his mind for the whole of the fifteen minutes I was gone, so eagerly he smiles as I return.

'I'm so sorry. I'm mistaken. Of course, it's not your sister but your uncle.' His eyes are liquid, his smile huge in his crumpled face. Is he telling me life holds endless promises? Neither of my two estranged uncles has set foot in the village for at least twenty years. I hurry on.

I have seen him around for as long as I can

remember. He must be in his fifties, but his grief, whatever causes it, his life, or mine, or the one he has created for me, is as bewildering and irresistible as a child's. He too must have seen me all his life, but he has never given in to the cosy chatter of village encounters. He either ignores me or expresses his deepest sympathy for tragedies he thinks have hit me. More often though, I arouse no compassion in him. Nothing. Nothing at all.

Many years ago, I was gone from the village, lured away to fight battles meant to retain the large country across the Mediterranean within the republic, and to give purpose to my life. Shortly after I returned, he rushed up to me near the grocer's and thanked me for having been there on that 'terrible day'.

'I will never forget what you and your father did,' he said.

'Yes, when was it? Time does fly, doesn't it?' I mumbled, trying to gather more details on my family's generosity. 'It's the least we could do in the circumstances,' I managed, striving to pull out unbroken threads of memories. But they remained in a tangled heap. When he had trotted up to me I had nearly hugged him, so familiar was his face. It was a part of my childhood landscape, as were the war memorial, the mountains in the west and the stooping figures of the old ladies I had been forced to kiss but whose full names I had never known. They had nicknames, sometimes first names and weird little anecdotes attached to them. Limpy was said to have been a beauty in her days and beaten up by a rival, which accounted for her limp. Greta (who after the kiss, touched my cheek with a crooked finger heavy with yellow stones) had soft white curls and, people whispered, a German father. I imagined the North Sea wind whirling around a tall silent man and a little girl with long sandy plaits as I stood there with the whispers in my ears, watching those curls.

When I came back after those years away, the

republic had lost Algeria and I, half an arm. Limpy and Greta's backs had arched a little further.

'Hello there. And how's Henri today? Isn't the wind freezing? Much worse than this time last year, isn't it? Oh well, must be off. Look after yourself,' they said, as if I'd been gone a week. And the old ladies, and the sight of the war memorial on the square, and the madman rushing up to me that day had cast a hazy pall over the years between the time I had left and the time I returned. The cracks in the walls had widened, bits of grey plaster had fallen off and shutters had closed. But plaster gets swept, and cracks and closed shutters go unnoticed. Or remain as unspoken as my absence.

The old ladies aren't around anymore. One after the other, they went missing. And as they went, as lightly as sparrows drop, gone were the nicknames, gone the funny stories. I had thought them here forever, like clouds that gather on the mountains when the wind dies out in the hot summer evenings. But they vanished, as did the young men whose names are inscribed on the war memorial, as do the events inside the vessel of the madman's mind. That day, shortly after I returned, I smiled and left him, the only memory I could unravel without a split or a knot reminding me he was not someone I normally talked to. I vowed to find out about that 'terrible day', mislaid in the turmoil of my life's past few years, but somehow, I never did. Or I don't think I did. For who was left to ask?

Some days, when I rush around busying myself with this and that, filling time with endless things that push and pull me here and there—must dash and buy some grated cheese, better mend that door, plane it down a bit, simply have to go and take these empty bottles down to the glass bin—I see him up to six or seven times. He stands in a doorway, often the one opposite my house, and stares towards the mountains. In winter, he wears brown corduroy trousers and a grey woollen coat with the collar turned up over his long straight hair; in summer, checked Bermuda shorts and moccasins. He is well dressed, even, to a certain extent, fashionably, as fashion goes in the village. I wonder who, if anyone, is behind the scene.

When dust and confetti swirl in the streets, he also dashes here and there, stiff and intent, from the market square to the public garden past the war memorial, the pillar rooted in the heart of the village. If I were a visitor, if I weren't aware of the patterns of his moves, I would think him a very busy man on those days when there's whirling and howling in the air. And when, up on someone's doorstep, he stands, arms like wooden sticks along his body, fists pressed against his legs, the tension on his face muscles and the flickering in his feverish eyes are signs he will soon be gone, as if on a mission of great urgency, usually to another nearby doorway. To and fro he darts, with the dried leaves and the empty cans and the plastic bags, like a lead soldier on parade gone awry.

But I wonder if anyone sees him. I don't think I have ever spoken to anyone about him, or ever known his name or ever asked anyone what it is. I forget him the minute I don't see him. The funny thing though, is no one has ever talked to me about him either. Perhaps they too forget about him as soon as he's out of sight. Or perhaps he has created tragedies for them they are not prepared to share, dreading who knows what. Let's face it, if I had to ask anyone about him I would have to mention his 'madness', to say something like, 'He's always sorry for some terrible thing that happened to me. The other day, he was sorry because of my sister. But I have no sister.' What if they said, 'Yes, *I too* am sorry.'? Or even worse, 'Oh was he? He was sorry for what happened to *my* sister.'? Perhaps he's everybody's fleeting secret, each of us wanting to remain the sole object of his grief and sympathy.

In the evening, my headache is gone and just before the grocer's closing time, I run out again to buy some peanuts. At the end of the street, beyond the motorway, I watch the gentle upward slope of the plain darkening. In the distance, the black-blue mountains stand heavy against the sky as it turns orange. Not wanting to trivialise the splendour of the transient sight into a weather forecast, I avoid the one or two familiar silhouettes on the pavement opposite. But they are quickening their steps as dusk shrouds the streets, vespers call and summon no one, and walls turn into tall grey barriers.

He is sitting on the step of a narrow house next to the grocer's, turned towards the spectacle, elbows on his knees, his chin resting in cupped hands. If I didn't know his pale, wizened face, I'd think he was a big tired child. Once perhaps, he let some woe seep from within through the surface of his face and he couldn't put it back inside. How many and whose tragedies has he gone through? I slacken my pace and try to meet his eye, to witness the intensity of the strange pain I sometimes bring out in him. But his eyes remain lost in despair, towards the mountains that reach out to the dark red tatters of the sky and melt onto the plain. Is he petrified at the wonder of the distant fading sight? Is he paralysed within the grief that creased his face when he saw me in the morning, aching for the ghosts in my life? Have I stopped existing inside his tortuous mind? But what about tomorrow? And the day after, and after?

Above the muffled roar of the motorway, only the swallows' swift circles and shrill whistles fill the setting darkness. I leave him, a mere hunched shadow. I hurry past the war memorial where his father's name, *his* name, may be inscribed, for all I know. There are so many, so many names. The old ladies' fathers' names. Their husbands' and their sons' names. They get washed away by time. Mine's not there though. I sometimes stop and check on my errands.

The streets are empty now, a playground open to everybody's fears. I lock myself up inside my home. As we all do in the village.

Ruins

'N'en poudès vous tourca lou darnié d'aquelo salouparié!'
'You can wipe your arse with this trash,' old Funel told the clerk at the *Mairie* of the town of S. as he flung his new ID card on the counter and banged his fist on top. 'You want to kill me once again? What kind of piece of crap is this that says I was born in a place I'd never set foot in until this year? And I've had a long life, young man. I'm eighty-one. What's written here is a lie and a disgrace. It's got nothing to do with me.' Old Funel grabbed the card and tore it to pieces before dropping the scraps on the floor and spitting on them. He turned to the clerk, looked him in the eye and added, 'You can stuff them bits of lies up your arse. I'm keeping my old card. Whether you like it or not, I was born in a village called B.' He kicked at the bits of paper on the floor, gave his cap a sharp tug over his forehead and stomped towards the exit. He held the door for his granddaughter Félicie and slammed it behind them.

Picture if you will that village called B., somewhere in the uplands of Provence where few travellers visit. Picture it as it was in the early 1970s. Let it come back to life up there on the plateau.

It is the kind of village a child would draw when asked to draw a village, with half a dozen pink houses along its main street, on either side of the church. A handful of others huddle behind the oval fountain and another few along by the paths that go up rocky grey-green mounds to the chapel and the sheep pen. When daylight lets go of the walls early, blue smoke whirls up the chimneys, a smell of burning logs drifts out into the night and the windows glow. As they are flung open to the spring, a ray of sun lands on a kitchen table, breaks into a thousand gems, and coffee shimmers in bowls. A puff of wind blows into the lilac, the scent wafts, and tipsy bees and butterflies swarm around the frame.

Step inside a house and place your elbows on a pink marble windowsill. Now rest your chin in the cup of your hands and hear the stream trickling down beyond the fountain. As the mist rises at dawn, gaze across the moor at the goats leaping over rocks and at the pensive sheep, fatter than the people, grazing in the meadows undulating in the currents of the breeze. In autumn, the mist sometimes lingers all day half-way up the blue mountains and the horizon reaches so far a short walk becomes a journey to a world elsewhere. But the air is so clear the next morning you feel it wouldn't take more than a flap of a wing to take you up to the edge of the horizon.

Listen! The church bells strike five and barely a minute later, three, six, twelve children come tumbling down the front door steps of the school, shrieking, kicking and blinking in the amber light of the late afternoon. Dogs yap behind boys who scamper up the path to fill pockets with stones in case, they shout, the wolf comes back. Girls shrug. Full of contempt, their eyes follow the boys and dogs till they disappear behind the juniper shrubs. They know better. They squat along the fountain wall and draw closer around the tall one. Old Funel's granddaughter has something to say. Last night, she heard her uncle tell her father the army would soon invade the plateau and chase them out of the village.

'It's a secret,' Félicie whispers to her friends, whose

hearts are beating fast.

'Is there a war?' a tiny wide-eyed girl asks.

'There are wars all around the world,' Félicie says looking in the distance. Hunting voles, a couple of buzzards are hovering.

The village has nothing to show for itself: no medieval castle, no Saracen tower, no golden triptych in its church. The stones Julius Caesar's soldiers cut and left, the people used over the centuries as foundations to their houses or to build their walls. It has a baker's, a grocer's and an inn. It is a village like any with saint, odd jobs for the bad and the mad, generational feuds. And like all villages in the country, a war memorial, with inscribed names of its young men killed in the First or the Second World Wars, rooted in its heart, opposite the church.

In the blizzards and the snowdrifts, you can't reach it for days and it is as lonely as a ship in a stormy, foamy ocean. And when the mistral blows, it howls across the moor, rushes along the troughs of stony drovers' paths and blusters over the roofs more wildly than elsewhere, as nothing stops its course here. Apart from under the lime tree on the church square and under the willows down along the stream, there isn't much shade to crawl to when the sun strikes, the trees sturdy but short, like the people. When evenings are warm, the elders sit under the lime tree, on the stone bench along the Funels' house. They watch the village and swap memories of droughts, fires and frosts, of long gone days. Rumours about the army chasing them out and settling on the plateau have reached their ears, too. But they shake their heads. On top of all the rest, they've been through two world wars. They all wheeze and cough and many aren't quite whole. 'But we're still here,' they say, 'and here to stay.'

In its heyday, the village had up to three hundred inhabitants. Now, in the early 1970s, just under eighty people—peasants and craftsmen, but mainly shepherds. A few farms and hamlets are scattered around the plateau, whose names, La Pié, Fouan Sant, San Peïre, haven't all got round to becoming French. Together with eight thousand goats and twenty thousand sheep, three hundred people live and work on the high plain all year. But in the summer months, three times as many frolic across the meadows—with the cousins and the grandchildren all up from the crowded, stifling coast towns and cities of the lowlands.

Little has changed since life made its slow way back after the Black Plague killed the whole population in the second half of the 14th century. It has remained a slow and often harsh life, whose events, big and small alike, depend mainly on the colour of the moon and the fancy of the wind and the rolling in or out of clouds.

Look at the village in the mid 1970s, surrounded by barbed wire, soundless apart from a shutter or two beating against a wall to the wind's tempo. Nobody in the streets. Windows are hollow eyes, doors are black holes. Roofs and chimneys have collapsed. Hour after hour, the clock on the bell tower says it's 12.20. A couple of vultures are circling, and the silence deepens.

You know at once its death was sudden and recent. It has no wild fig trees growing in the roof holes, no creepers pushing through tiles, no brambles shooting out from walls, not a trace of the slow decay that gnaws at buildings when men abandon them in search of better lives. But though it died a sudden death, there is no crack in the ground, no broken chair or plate, no doll lying in the street, no house half-buried in the earth. No earthquake shook the rocks.

Now walk the silent streets and let your eyes glide along the walls still standing. They are riddled with holes, bullet holes. Step inside a house. Swaying in the draughts, tatters of flowery wallpaper brush your cheek. You trip on broken tiles, look up, but see no fallen tree through the ceiling, no trace of lightning, just bits of sky. The village died a violent, unnatural death. And then you notice the beams are gone and the fireplace and the carved doors. Step out and walk to the church. Up the bell tower is a patch of deep blue. The two bells are gone as well. The village was looted. Turn around away from the church. The war memorial is gone.

And yet, no foreign army attacked, bombed or plundered. Let darkness stretch across the plateau and shroud the village. The wind and the wolves are howling in the night.

With the loss of Algeria in 1962, during the Cold War, the French army lost its desert grounds. In the solitude of the high plain, amid the moor and pasture land, the army found the huge expanse where, on its own soil and on a grand scale, it could test its long-range weapons and rehearse its wars at peace. In the early 1970s, the plateau and nearby mountains became the largest military camp and shooting range in Europe. The village, its hamlets and farms, were included in the camp, and on 4th August 1970, they lost their legal existence. The last village fête was held in August, 1972. The post office and the school were closed for good in June, 1973, followed by the baker's, the grocer's and the inn at the end of the year. Barbed wire was placed around the village, and the expulsions began. The last inhabitants of B., the twenty-two people who could not or would not leave the village, were expelled on 7th June, 1974. Water and electricity were cut off for good on that spring day and at 12.20 p.m., time stopped. It was decreed the village did not exist anymore. Its name was wiped off along the roads and appeared on no new map. All those born in the village were now officially born in the town of S. forty kilometres to the south.

The army had offered resettlement in a new village they would build, complete with cemetery, church and sports centre. Only those who had no choice, the Funels and two other families, accepted. On the outskirts of S., they found a muddy building site and waited a year before they could move into unfinished little white boxes, thin-walled houses along the bypass. The war memorial followed in an army truck and was embedded in front of the little boxes. And then the bones from the old cemetery were brought and thrown into a communal grave behind the memorial.

Fred, Félicie's father, often stays awake till dawn in his small bedroom in the thin-walled house, staring at the lights flickering on the ceiling as lorries rumble past on the bypass. He mulls over his time across the Mediterranean Sea. He was eighteen when shipped off to Algeria as a conscript to fight to retain the country within the republic. He and his mates obeyed their superiors, learned how to pack things fast, run in the sand, grit their teeth and shoot. Before lights were out in the stifling dorms, they played cards. After a year of shooting at strangers' chests and stumbling on corpses with slit throats, they played cards less at night and talked. Some began to wonder what they were doing. Others said they had no reason, no right even to be there, fighting those who wanted their country to be independent. Fred listened and wasn't sure. One night, he was awakened by screams he attributed to a jackal.

'A jackal? Don't be a fool,' a mate told him. 'They've caught a couple. They're doing what's necessary.'

'Necessary?'

'Yes. They do what it takes to get them to talk. What do you think?' When a few nights later he heard those screams again, he packed his rucksack fast, stepped out of the barracks and walked away in the desert. He didn't get far. He was caught and locked up for a year. Decades on, Fred still can't get over the fact that if Algeria had remained French, they might still be living in B. in their old pink house. He thinks he was a pawn from start to finish, and when he looks back to that time and contemplates the present, he cannot go to sleep.

'B. vou pas mouri,' 'B. doesn't want to die'. 'The army is chasing us. Help us'. When they heard the government declare the plateau was a virtually uninhabited, worthless wilderness and would be handed over to the army, the villagers wrote little notices they stuck on their walls. The shepherds blocked the road with their sheep and the peasants with their tractors. But except for weddings, funerals and the fête, the villagers were not used to getting together, standing up for themselves and speaking out. All day and most days of their lives, out on the moor, in the stony fields or their workshops, they were alone, and words were tools they scarcely used.

A coach full of young pacifists came from Paris. They put up large banners across the main street, got their photos in the local and national papers, were seen for a minute or two on the television news expressing outrage, and left. And a coach full of young communists came from Paris, put up banners and made speeches, and left. When it became clear the plans might go ahead, the headmaster tried to organise the villagers to resist. He wrote letters on their behalf to the *Préfet* and the *Sénateur* inviting them to listen to what they had to say. The *Préfet* and the *Sénateur* sent a couple of their counsellors up to the village. In the packed main room of the *Mairie*, the men in dark suits pulled papers and maps out of their briefcases and waved them about.

'The commies are just round the corner. We need to be ready for them when they come,' they said.

'And anyway, let's face it, your way of life is doomed,' they added.

'But you needn't worry. The army will build a new village for you, complete with church and sports centre,' they said.

'And the elders will be allowed to stay in the village till they die,' they added.

And more men came up.

'It'll be good for trade. They'll eat and drink and buy,' the shopkeepers from the towns nearby said.

'It'll create new jobs,' the mayors from the nearby villages claimed.

'Wildlife will be preserved,' the hunters' associations assured.

'They'll buy property,' the property owners and the estate agents and the notaries repeated.

All of them said, 'You'll get a good deal negotiating with the army.'

The villagers listened to them. When they were gone, the villagers could hear the wind rustling through the lime tree leaves again, the water flowing from the fountain, the lambs bleating in the meadows, the owl hooting in the willows down along the stream. And they wondered how much longer they would hear those sounds. They gathered in the smoky stillness of the Golden Pheasant at night, and sat there, hunched. They drank and stared inside their empty glasses and filled them up again. They'd glimpsed at the glitter of city neon lights shining in the young men's eyes and guessed their heads would spin with the strange lure of cinemas and big shops and fast cars tearing along motorways. And they knew that a thought—never voiced—was forming: 'We'll get a good deal if we negotiate.' And the negotiations started. Even on a warm evening, the bench under the lime tree along the Funels' house remained empty and at night, the inn was dark. Now and then, you'd hear a lamb bleat and see a lonely silhouette run up to the pen or, when vespers called at dusk, another steal inside the church.

But on the evening of 7th June, 1974, all were gone. There were two thousand, six hundred soldiers on the plateau. The shock of blasts and heavy gunfire rumbled and ran freely across the moor. Military planes tore the sky. And in the village, the army started perfecting its urban warfare and rehearsing its guerrilla wars. Bullets whistled in the air and firebombs and shells fell on the roofs of the pink houses. No one mentioned the village anymore.

Night and day, tanks and jeeps and lorries packed with young men in full battle gear roared up and down the road the army had swiftly built across the plateau. The villagers always sped along the road. They never slowed, never looked to the bell tower beyond the willow trees. Yet strange visions forced their way through their rolled-up windows. Tense young men, standing in front of the church under their green helmets, shouting orders. Or kneeling, in firing position, intent at aiming straight, grimacing over their rifles under the lime tree. Shooting at the windows of the inn and the school gate. On their knees and elbows, crawling in dry mud around the oval fountain as bullets hissed over their heads. Sinking in the rubble of roofs and pink walls collapsing. Crying in the dust clouds of chimneys crumbling and shutters falling. Yelling, running away from their phoney enemies. Shining eyes darting through the slits in the heads of the caterpillar tracks near the chapel. Tracking foes they never saw amid the juniper, the lavender and the thyme as cannons shot and fired and stopped and soon went off again.

When the visions got too clear, when the furious dogged attacks against phantom targets got too loud and resounded in his head, Fred sang old songs at the top of his voice as he drove. He sang to cover the blasts and keep the tense young men at bay. But Félicie knew the louder her father sang, the heavier the silence would be at home that night. He hardly spoke, never went back or forth in time, simply stated the day's chores.

'Look, there's a funny old village over there,' Félicie blurted one day from the back of the car. 'It's a mirage, isn't it?' she added with the cheekiness of a teenager.

Her father pulled over by the side of the road, turned around, slapped her hard across the face and said, 'And this, my girl, is a gust of mistral blowing in the mirage.'

The villagers had let a lid fall over their anger. They'd locked their past inside their memories and grief, alongside their shame and guilt. They soldiered on inside their new homes, and pretended. They pretended they couldn't hear the blasts and didn't know their village had always been there, beyond the willow trees. They pretended they still owned the landscape, and had no past. And their silence deepened.

Nothing favours the growth of phantoms as silence. With every blow, something in you dies, a trace of innocence, a ray of hope, a tiny dream. And then a phantom comes along, that tinge of fear or grief or guilt. It settles in you, inside a fold where it can hide and from then on, lurks in the dark. Those phantoms hate light. They choose the dead of night to make their din, which only you can hear. They clang and bang and clank. They come awake when least expected.

Put yourself inside their shoes, for a minute or two, inside a shepherd's, the baker's or postman's shoes. Tie up your laces and walk along a busy, noisy street in the city. You feel a breeze upon your face that carries on its tail a whiff of thyme. And for a moment of bliss, you're up there, on the plateau, in B., under the lime tree, on a warm spring day. But then you know you're not, and never will be, and you're done. A phantom is awake. It strikes a little chord that echoes around your stomach as though an organ were playing in a cave. Another day, you hear about people somewhere, united, refusing to let go of their land or village, up in arms to save them. And a phantom's pricked you here and there, injected a liquid inside your veins that ripples through your body, leaving you numb. On every 7th June they rattle in your chest those phantoms, go on a rampage in your stomach, hit and knock inside your heart.

But not a word from you about all this. Before they reach your lips, words get strangled in your throat. And as those phantoms don't like words and live in fear of being named, the less they're spoken of, the noisier and sturdier they are. As time goes by and silence grows, they thrive and get the upper hand over your life. And anyway, what is it you would say? That since you left the plateau, your days have shrunk? That when you lived up there, each day was like the sky, huge and forever changing? And each night was fully dark and silent but now, it wraps its greyish folds around your hazy days and hums and hums? That you can't tell one season from another? That like a cut off limb, the lost village leaves you with a phantom pain?

They'd laugh. They might start whispering about old Funel, about the night his granddaughter Félicie found him on the edge of his bed in the room they shared in their small new house, shortly after his outburst at the *Mairie* of S. In his Sunday best, he was clutching the handle of an old brown leather suitcase at his feet.

'I'm going home,' he said. 'They're coming to fetch me to take me home. I'm going back to B.' He wouldn't move, wouldn't let go of his suitcase, and they never got another word from him, just, 'They're coming to take me home. I'm going back to B.' They came and took him to a home down in a coast town where he refused to unpack, hardly spoke or ate, and where he died, barely a month later.

So you keep quiet and, standing at the edge of your life, let the phantoms have a jolly time.

One day, the bombings, shots and blasts stopped in and around the village. The Cold War and the Red Scare were over. The army had other wars to rehearse, wars for which the village wouldn't do. They searched the mountains to find the narrow valley where they could build a dried mud village on a slope and start practising before deployment in the east.

Ivy began to slowly grip the stones, nettles to push through the cracks, brambles to tumble over the pink marble windowsills, wild rose to climb up staircases that led to the sky. Foxes wriggled through the holes in the rusting barbed wire and settled behind the altar in the church. Golden grass snakes coiled on the soft moss inside the fountain. Hanging upside down, families of bats slept in the narrow cupboards in the walls. And as the moor was claiming back the village, the remnants of its past life sank deeper inside the well of the old villagers' memories until, a little more swiftly than their parents, they went, taking their phantoms along with them. And the willows grew.

Open to the winds, the houses had visitors, lost hikers, curious travellers, wild boar hunters, adventurous lovers. They tripped on bullets, sardine tins, rusted beer cans. They got bitten by vipers, fell through rotten staircases, got hit on their heads by a stone falling from a lintel. And they blamed the army. In 2005, the army declared that the village was dangerous and too expensive to keep, and they would tear it down. Bulldozers were to go into action.

When she reads about the plan to raze the village, Félicie Funel is sitting behind the cash desk in the supermarket where she's been working for the last twenty years. These are the best moments of her day; just after lunch, she can sit back, close her eyes for a minute and, if no customer appears, snatch the paper from the rack. She can read about the wars around the world, glance at her horoscope on the page before last. But she doesn't get to her horoscope. When she sees 'B., the forgotten village on the C. plateau, is to be demolished', she gasps and stuffs the paper inside her bag as a customer approaches.

Félicie has no phantoms, no phantom pain, but she has memories. The night she found old Funel sitting on his bed in their small room, cap screwed on his head, clutching his suitcase and repeating, 'I'm going back to B.' over and over, she knelt in front of him, put her hands on his lap and said, 'No, no, Granddad, you can't go back, we're here now.' But he didn't hear her. She tried to loosen his grip on the handle of the suitcase, but his fingers, the three he had left, were as hard as iron pliers. He was looking past her, staring at something invisible behind her, beyond the wall. There was a gleam inside his eyes she had never seen before. As if he'd left the room and wandered to a place that existed on no map, peopled with ghosts. And over there, she thought that night, shivering with fear, he's alone with them. As she sits behind the till, that night comes back as clear as a clear night on the plateau.

She'll go on Sunday. She's never been back, but now's the time. The village was foreclosed and forbidden, and then forsaken. But forgotten, as they write? No. Not yet. Not quite. But if they wipe what's left off the face of the earth, then it will be—for good.

The plateau is windswept. She drives slowly and after the last bend, sees the silver swell of the willow boughs swaying. The top of the bell tower appears, a lost raft in the swell. She pulls over, rolls her window down and a gust of mistral blows in, reminding her of her father's slap when she mocked the silence her parents had fallen into and imposed around them. But her father was right. The village is no mirage. And by trespassing and treading on its paths she will defy the army and its lies.

She crawls under the rusted barbed wire. The wind is hissing down the main street. She treads slowly, glances at the skeletons of the disembowelled houses, at the bullet-riddled walls. She reaches the square. Its rough, rugged, wasted beauty leaves her stunned. At first she cannot tell what shapes the villagers hewed from those the wind and hail carved. But then she makes out the curving bridge down there, the rocky path to the sheep pen, the oval fountain. She walks to the fountain, slides down along the soft mossy wall, sits on the tender grass, and listens to the swishing, fluttering, squeaking of snakes, thrushes, badgers teeming all around. The clock on the bell tower says it's 12.20 as it did the day they left, over thirty years ago. Huge boughs of the lime tree are nestling inside the caved-in roof of her house. And along the wall, two thick slabs of stone are left askew. The bench, broken. It was one of the last lies they told her granddad; that he, and all the elders, could live here and sit on the bench on warm nights, till they died. A new village, ready for them when they came. Wealth and prosperity to the area thanks to the camp and its thousands of soldiers.

And what about the old one, the biggest lie of all, '*dulce et decorum est pro patria mori*'? Did her grandfather believe, when the tocsin sounded across the plateau and he and his friends marched off with a flower in the muzzle of their rifles? Did he believe when he was trapped in the rat-infested trenches of Verdun? When he saw his friends blown to bits? When he helped dig holes for the nameless? When he came back and learned that six of them had been killed? Did they think '*dulce*', those young men who didn't lose their lives but an eye, an arm, a leg? Did they think '*decorum*', these gaunt, broken men who came back from the front wheezing and limping, and who howled in their sleep till they died?

Félicie hid under her sheet, shut her eyes tight and pressed her hands over her ears when her granddad howled in the middle of the night. No one in the house ever mentioned the howling, or the war. But she overheard snatches and worked out that the three toes he'd lost had been frozen in the trenches and the two fingers, crushed by a falling wooden box packed with shells. There was one thing she knew: until that day in June, 1974, when he had to hand over the key to their house to a silent officer, her granddad's mind was sound and clear. He lost it all the day he had to leave the village, when phantoms took over.

It had taken more than a thousand years for the village to be the kind a child would draw if asked to draw a village. It probably took a ninny in his office of the Ministry of Defence in Paris no more than an hour or two to conclude the report that included the village in the camp and so the displacement of eighty people. A trifle for the Ministry, not even collateral damage. The ninny in his office could have concluded differently. It didn't matter to him. He could have suggested that the limit of the camp be placed a hundred meters further to the west. But he didn't. And his report accomplished what the Black Plague, cholera epidemics, WW1, the Spanish flue, WW2, and the rural exodus didn't. Life may have trickled out of the village eventually, but slowly, slowly, in a century or two. But then, maybe it wouldn't have.

'*Défense d'entrer. Terrain militaire. Tirs en cours. Danger de mort.*' Every fifty meters, a signpost reminds you the plateau is the huge forbidden stage set for the dummy run of bloody wars that will leave more nameless, broken bodies lying in the ruins of more villages thousands of miles away. In that deadly solitude, Félicie looks in the rear-view mirror as she drives away and sees it dwindling, her village, a tiny dot and, after a bend, not even that. It's sliding down a shaft of dimming light, slipping into darkness, melting like a sand castle in dying waves, into nothingness. Whatever bits of village life the elders held inside the nooks and crannies of their memories died with them. The fragments of that life her parents have retained, they keep locked up and won't, or cannot share. And now, when she stumbles on a memory of B., she finds it blurred and faded. Razed to the ground or not, her village will soon be forgotten, unheard of, as invisible as if it had never existed. The unbearable thought.

To save something, even a scrap, before ivy, moss and bramble cover up all trace, what can be done? What can be done before the sun, rain, wind and time do their wiping jobs, leaving a few scattered stones like bones vultures have stripped of flesh? Before its ruins sink into the moor and oblivion grinds it back to dust? Before it goes forever, out of sight and out of memory, what can be done? What rampart can there be against a death assured except, perhaps, a story told?

So Félicie sat and wrote.

Lightning Source UK Ltd.
Milton Keynes UK
UKHW040625251020
372194UK00001B/8